Whose dark or troubled mind will you step into next? Detective or assassin, victim or accomplice? How can you tell reality from delusion when you're spinning in the whirl of a thriller, or trapped in the grip of an unsolvable mystery? When you can't trust your senses, or anyone you meet; that's when you know you're in the hands of the undisputed masters of crime fiction.

Writers of the greatest thrillers and mysteries on earth, who inspired those that followed. Their books are found on shelves all across their home countries – from Asia to Europe, and everywhere in between. Timeless tales that have been devoured, adored and handed down through the decades. Iconic books that have inspired films, and demand to be read and read again. And now we've introduced Pushkin Vertigo Originals – the greatest contemporary crime writing from across the globe, by some of today's best authors.

So step inside a dizzying world of criminal masterminds with **Pushkin Vertigo**. The only trouble you might have is leaving them behind.

FRÉDÉRIC DARD

PUSHKIN VERTIGO

THE WICKED GO TO HELL

TRANSLATED FROM THE FRENCH BY DAVID COWARD

Pushkin Vertigo
71–75 Shelton Street
London, WC2H 9JQ

Original text © 1956 Fleuve Editions,
département d'Univers Poche, Paris

First published in French as *Les Salauds vont en enfer* in 1956

Translation © David Coward, 2016

First published by Pushkin Vertigo in 2016

1 3 5 7 9 8 6 4 2

ISBN 978 1 782271 96 3

Text designed and typeset by Tetragon, London

Printed and bound by CPI Group (UK) Ltd, Croydon CRO 4YY

www.pushkinpress.com

To Christine Garnier, who liked the play
To Robert Hossein, who directed the film
To Armand de Caro, who wanted the novel

There are times when whether a man's a cop or a crook means nothing, times when it ceases to matter which side of the fence he's on. There aren't any fences any more! We're just a couple of guys! Two poor saps adrift in the lowest depths of hell!

I remember that the sky that morning was white. You know, the sort of sky on which you'd like to scrawl portents in feathery writing! A sky that would stir up humankind to fashion the world anew... or to put an end to it once and for all!

Paris had drooped like a faded flag on the front of a public building. The weather was warm and joyless.

I gave a sigh and ran two at a time up the steps which led to the imposing and very dirty entrance of the Service.

Once you're through the porch, the smell of the world outside slips away from you, along with some of its colour. You begin moving in a bizarre element which is a little nebulous, a tinge acrid and very uncertain.

This is down to the fact that here in this building things happen... How can I explain it?... Let's just say things, *and leave it at that!... Things which are not known to the man in the street—which is as well for his peace of mind—and of which we never speak, which is as well for ours.*

Because before telling you any more, I must admit something: we do actually have a conscience. But it is so deeply buried under our DUTY that we are practically unable to hear its voice when, as happens with everyone's conscience, it starts to protest.

It's better that way, believe me.

When I walked into the Old Man's office, he was ensconced, almost lying, in his swivel chair with his hands clasped over his stomach. His eyes were half-closed and he seemed to be meditating or listening... My arrival did not disturb his concentration. With a brief nod he motioned me to take a seat... Or rather the seat, since there were only two in the Old Man's office: his and the Client's. It is an office where people come, in theory, alone. For the Old Man is much too focused to have several people in at a time.

So I sat down and I waited.

When you're sitting opposite someone like him, the only thing you want is to be elsewhere.

All of us here are scared of him. And we do not forgive him for creating such fear in us because no one can explain it. He is cordial to everyone, kindly even. He has a fifty-something's face, placid if a little too lined. There is sadness in his eyes, which should earn him sympathy. But the overall effect conveys something which makes the blood run cold. I think it must come from its being so calm. A man is intended to live, to do things, to talk... But he doesn't talk much and when he does speak his voice always sounds unfeeling. He never says anything that concerns himself, personally. You are left with the depressing sense that his person and his personality have never been introduced to each other.

After a brief moment, I also started listening. Curious noises were coming from a room nearby. There was a muffled thud and then what could have been a groan. It did not take me long to understand. I'd heard that kind of sound somewhere before.

Some of our colleagues were "attending" to some guy and, if I could trust what I was hearing, they weren't going easy on him.

*Eventually, the Old Man sat up. His chair creaked. He winked,
which was his way of saying hello. Then, gesturing towards the source
of the sounds, he shook his head and murmured:*

"He won't talk."

*I had no idea whom he meant but even without knowing the
patient in question, I was thinking the same thing. There was a
kind of rhythm to the blows and the cries which followed them. Now,
rhythm is a form of habit and you don't break a man who has got
into the painful habit of being hit.*

*As if he'd been following my train of thought, the Old Man said:
"Will he?"*

*His expression seemed more disillusioned than usual. Because
of those sad blue eyes of his, you feel you should ask him what is
wrong. But then you notice those two powerful hands, as still as two
wild animals stalking prey, and you say nothing.*

*"Men who yowl never talk," he said. "From the start they settle
into pain and thereafter you can go on hitting them but they just
put up the shutters."*

*I knew all that. I gave the nod of agreement which he was expect-
ing and he went on:*

*"It's the fifth time he's been questioned. It's four times too many!
From the first session I knew it was a waste of time... Nothing! The
hell with him!"*

*He reached out his hand for the internal phone. He pressed a
button and almost instantaneously the "noises" stopped.*

A breathless voice growled: "Hello!"

"Go easy," sighed the chief. "You're overdoing it!"

*He did not wait for the man at the other end to react. With a
circular, elegant movement of his hand, he hung up, taking care not
to snag the wire between the cradle and the receiver.*

"Just like kids," he sighed. "You give them a drum and they're not happy until they've stove it in."

He fell silent, listening hard, as sharp-eared as a sick man.

After a while, he reached for a box of matches.

"Listen, Mérins, it was because of this customer that I sent for you."

I did not react.

"We find ourselves in a difficult position," he went on.

At that moment there was a long scream. It was very close. It was an inhuman sound… Whoever uttered it wasn't thinking about his image.

"Just like him, then," murmured the Old Man.

His lip curled in an unpleasant smile. But he's no sadist, as he proved by picking up the phone again and ordering the interrogation to be stopped. After this he seemed calmer, almost relaxed.

He started talking again, about the customer, gesturing towards the right-hand wall each time he spoke, as if the bare bricks had the power to conjure up the punter about whom all I knew was the way he screamed.

"The man's a spy. He was arrested as he was breaking into a safe in the main lab at Saclay. He had cut the wire to the alarm system but security had connected a second, less obvious one."

At this point the customer next door started to become a little more tangible in my mind. He ceased to be a groan and began to acquire a definite shape.

"He wasn't acting on the spur of the moment."

The Old Man's voice had reverted to its mechanical rhythm, which was as impersonal as the ticking of a watch.

"He wasn't acting on his own behalf either! Behind him there's an organization and we have to find out what it is! Since all the methods we have used on him have failed, I have no choice but to fall back on the last resort."

My heart missed a beat and I realized that he was going to ask me to do something special.

And I was right!

"Our man has got to escape and escape he will... with you!"

He looked at me to see my reaction but I'd long been used to letting the sky fall on me without batting an eyelid.

"We'll lock you both up in the same jail cell... a tough one... the sort of place that gives kindly old ladies the shivers. The pair of you will escape!

"You'll try to hole up somewhere and you'll wait. The breakout will be big news. The head of the organization, knowing that his man has escaped, will want to get him back... At some point or other, he'll break cover... Then, when you've got your hands on him..."

He made a chopping motion with the side of his hand. The gesture meant death.

"Got it?"

I had some difficulty unsticking my tongue from the roof of my mouth.

"Yes, chief!"

"Cigarette?" he said.

"No thanks."

"So you really don't smoke!" He went on: "You'll have plenty of problems. First, you'll have to gain the man's confidence, because he'll smell a rat. Wolves are good at sniffing out rats. Anyway, you'll do your best. You're smart!"

The hardest thing remained to be said and he didn't dare say it. You could sense a vague diffidence in him about using the crude words, the grubby but precise, tough words.

He opened the box of matches and started fiddling with it. The thin matchsticks spilt out onto his blotting pad. The Old Man picked them up one by one as he spoke. This gave him an excuse for not looking me in the eye.

"Your second problem: the escape... Keep telling yourself, old son, that you're acting unofficially."

He repeated the word, spelling it out with great vehemence:

"Un-off-icia-lly! The minute you leave this office I shall disown you! You know what that means?"

Sure, I knew. He couldn't help taking a sly sideways look at me.

"If you run into trouble, I won't be able to lift a finger to help you, especially since your escape won't happen without breakages...

"Look at me!"

I looked at him.

"Nobody's going to worry if there's blood on the wall... You got that?"

His blue eyes made me uncomfortable. But mine couldn't have been exactly restful either, because he looked away.

"Anyway, there it is," he said with a sigh. "I hope the good Lord above will be with you... Either the good Lord... or the Devil, because hell is where you're going!"

PART I

The Beast

1

The corridor was in the form of a T.

To left and right, the metal-barred cell doors ran in a row with depressing uniformity. You looked along the line of them and the bars played tricks with the eyes.

The place was badly lit by a transom window situated high up, which was darkened by bars and nearby walls. There was the sound of footsteps. They were amplified by the echo of the corridor. Hands stuck out from all the cells as they reached for the bars. Pale faces appeared between the hands. It was an eerie spectacle, for the darkness obscured the rest of the bodies so that the prisoners looked like the heads of fallen angels nailed to a backdrop of night, with their hands for wings.

The escort appeared. Four men. Martin, the warder who limped, hobbled briskly a little apart from the group, his pass key swinging as he advanced. The two new men, handcuffed together, walked abreast, like a pair of yoked oxen, while the Bull brought up the rear, a pleasant smile etched on his lips under the flower he perpetually chewed.

As they passed the other gawping prisoners, he got a buzz out of rapping the knuckles showing white around the bars of the cell doors. And all the while without losing his smile or breaking his mayoral step.

When they reached the end of the corridor, that is, of the second branch of the T, Martin opened a door and stood back to let the new arrivals past. The two men stepped into the cell, the first holding his manacled hand behind his back so as not to impede his companion.

Martin slammed the door shut behind them. The noise was almost physically painful. It was the sound of freedom imploding.

Both newcomers stood motionless, again like two oxen, unmoving and dejected, looking around the cell where a third prisoner was already seated. Unaccustomed to the semi-dark, they could barely make him out.

"Turn round!" barked the Bull.

Unprotesting, they turned, slowly, taking care not to become snarled up in their chain.

The chief warder seemed even bigger on the other side of the bars. He filled out his clothes like some voluminous, flabby, vaguely repulsive thing: he looked like a heap of entrails.

"Hands!"

Each of the newcomers raised the hand that was chained. The Bull put his own large fists, which were swollen and smooth-skinned, through the bars and unlocked their manacles.

"I'm taking your bracelets off," he said. "If it were up to me, I'd leave them on… For a couple of jailbirds like you two, I think bracelets have got more style."

He gave a ponderous chuckle.

"Still," he sighed, "regulations is regulations."

For a moment he stared at the two inmates. Both men's faces were covered with bruises. The prisoner on his right had one eye half-shut because his eyebrow was gashed. The upper lip of the prisoner on his left was split.

The Bull sucked on his flower. A ripple of mirth seemed to rise up from his abdomen. It shook his entire body.

"Well now, boys," he said, "looks like somebody's been trying to rearrange your faces for you!"

The two men still did not move. They both seemed numb. Their dazed condition pushed their broad shoulders down.

"You can rub your wrists," the Bull obligingly informed them.

And when the newcomers did not take up the suggestion:

"Don't be shy," the chief warder persisted. "They all do it."

His eyes filled with spite. That is, the gleam in them became more insistent and they seemed whiter, and stared more fixedly.

The two men did not react.

"Suit yourselves, scumbags."

Martin walked away slowly down the corridor… One by one, the hands of the other prisoners disappeared from the bars and their pale faces melted into the darkness.

"Right, I still got a couple of things to tell you," said the chief warder. "Two important things, things you'll find useful. First, my name is Duroc, but you won't need to use it since all the guys here call me the Bull… You'll soon find out why."

He gave another of his glutinous laughs.

"The second thing: I don't like people who don't toe the line… Or put it this way: they don't like me.

"When I see guys like you two walk through the door, with their mugs already mangulated, well, I can't help myself."

Suddenly he pushed one arm roughly into the cell and achieved the difficult feat of hitting the men with the flat and then the back of his hand… He must have perfected the trick long ago because he performed it at incredible speed.

"I just can't help myself," he said in a soft, piping voice which contrasted comically with his corpulence. "It's just like when a dog sees a tree… it makes him want to take a leak.

And when I see men like you two, it makes me want to slap somebody… Have you got that?"

When both men said nothing, he screamed:

"Have you got that?"

"Me, I got the message loud and clear," muttered the smaller of the pair.

"Same here," said the other. "On that I got no complaints."

The Bull spat out his flower into the cell. He poked the tip of his disgusting tongue over his greedy lips.

"You seem like a couple of nice, wised-up young fellas… Well. We'll see!… We'll see…"

He started to turn away, then stopped.

"Lemme put you in the picture about one other thing: the guy in the corner can't talk… A deaf mute who killed his wife. I hope you all get along together. Just in case it don't work for the three of you, I got to tell you that house rules don't allow fights!"

He stared at them grimly, one after the other.

"Be good!"

He turned on his heel and walked off, whistling under his breath.

2

When the Bull had gone, the two new men remained standing side by side for a moment, without looking at each other. Then there was a kind of click of release. Time, which had been flowing over them without intruding on their consciousness, suddenly jolted them out of their prisoner's stupor and swept them up on its aimless way. They looked at each other closely for the first time, sizing each other up with fierce interest, like two animals who come face to face. Eventually, one of them—the one with the half-closed eye—gave a shrug. He looked round the cell. There were three hinged cots, each with a straw mattress and a blanket. The prisoner who couldn't speak occupied the farthest one.

The man with the split lip gestured towards the two unclaimed pallets.

"The only freedom we've got left," he said sneeringly, "is the freedom to choose which bed we have. Do you prefer one or the other?"

The other man flopped onto the cot that was nearest.

"We're not on a train," he sighed. "Here, it don't matter whether you want facing or back to the engine…"

He stretched out his legs and put both arms under his head.

"The name's Frank," he said after a moment. "Frank somebody, but that don't matter any more. I left my surname at the door… in the register… What's great about this place is that you don't need any papers saying who you are…"

His companion lay down on his stomach on the remaining bed. He stretched his arms along the sides of his body and kept his head buried in the evil-smelling mattress. It stank of sweat and dirt. It was acrid, pervasive, but not so very unpleasant when you got used to it… The trick was getting used to it.

"Mine's Hal," he said after a while.

His voice was muffled, barely audible.

"Let's leave it at that. No need for introductions," he added. "It'll come down to first names soon enough anyway, so we might as well make a start now."

Frank said:

"Thanks. And same goes for me."

The mute had not shown any reaction. He was still curled up on his bed watching his new cellmates with an air of resignation.

He was a small man, thin and sallow, with grey hair, a large raven's-beak nose and thick tufts for eyebrows.

Slowly, Hal heaved himself onto one elbow and winked at him. He felt as abandoned as a dead body.

"Anyhow," he said aloud, "we'll feel drained today, but tomorrow we'll start getting used to it…"

Frank gave a start.

"Used to what?"

His companion waved one hand vaguely.

"You know… everything! To jail… to the whole deal… I'll get used to you and you'll get used to me… Isn't life just grand?"

"That's news to me…"

"What's news to you?… The idea of getting used to me?"

"You bet!" said Frank venomously. "Also the idea that life is just grand. There's days when I look up and see that life's got a face that's as friendly as a toad!"

He pointed to the mute man.

"There, that's what your precious life looks like, you moron!"

Instead of getting angry, Hal smiled. The mute made an effort to understand because he'd seen that they were talking about him. But he couldn't work out these new men. They weren't the usual run of jailbirds.

"This your first time inside?" asked Hal.

"What's it to you?"

"Oh, nothing, nothing at all."

"So why ask?"

"You know, talking without saying anything is another of those habits you got to get into. Take the weather. You can't count on the weather to keep the conversation going. The weather! Boy, the weather has played a big part in my life. And that's a fact. I was a truck driver... But now..."

He stretched and gave a moan of pleasure.

"...I've got the weather off my back now. Come rain or shine, I don't give a damn! Not a damn! Not a single damn!"

He'd shouted loud enough to strain his voice box. Frank watched him out of the corner of his eye. He didn't feel threatened, just curious.

Tears were streaming down Hal's battered cheeks.

He hiccuped and said:

"Say, can you believe that at this very moment there are guys out there tapping their barometers or listening to the weather forecast on the radio?"

Frank got up and walked a few paces to the cell door. His hands gripped the bars hungrily as he looked out.

The corridor was empty. He could hear other prisoners whispering to each other.

"Nope," he said. "There's nothing out there! Out there don't exist any more! All there is now is bars… That's God's truth… Bars have sprung up all round me like a forest of iron! And I'm alone! All alone!…"

He leant his head against the bars.

"All alone?" murmured Hal diffidently. "What about me, then?"

"Oh, you…"

"What do you mean by that?"

"You don't matter."

"Thanks a million!"

"What difference does it make to me that you're here, eh? Maybe you think I'm interested in your case?"

He took three paces, which brought him to the foot of his cellmate's makeshift bed.

He stared at Hal's face, which was puffy from the beating he'd been given. Hal had a shock of thick, brown hair, light-coloured eyes, more grey than blue, and vigorous features.

"Anyway, you've got an ugly mug!" he added.

It was Hal's turn to scrutinize his cellmate. Through the tears misting his eyes, he made out his mean face leaning over him. Frank had light-brown hair. He was fine-featured and his eyes were blue, quick and intense. Hal reckoned that with both eyes in good shape, Frank would be a good-looking man.

"You heard what the screw said," he muttered. "No fights in here. You've got the creeps, that's normal. But it's not a reason for taking it out on me!"

The arrival of the Bull temporarily suspended their spat.

"Listen up, you two!" he said. "I forgot to say one thing: you mustn't use the bedding to hang yourselves with!… House rules don't allow it!"

He gave a laugh, mightily pleased with the witticism.

"Seeing you two, no one could say you look as fresh as daisies. My, it must have been some roughing-up they dished out! I tell you, that's one party I'm real sorry I missed! Just look at you, so beat up you look like brothers!"

He had replaced the first little flower with another one, freshly picked. The one he was chewing on now was a nasturtium. A yellow nasturtium, delicate and shaped like the very small horn of an ancient gramophone.

"I'll make you piss blood," he promised as he walked away.

Frank sighed:

"Brothers…"

The word had shocked him. He sat on the end of Hal's cot.

"Lemme see!" he barked.

"See what?"

"Your cuts and grazes."

"You want to know what yours look like?"

"That's part of it."

"You want to use me as a mirror, is that it?"

"Basically, yes!"

Hal gave a derisive laugh:

"Why not show me yours?… May I?"

Without waiting for a reply, he reached out one hand towards Frank's face. He touched the cuts and abrasions. He felt stickiness. Frank yowled with pain and pushed Hal savagely away. Hal fell backwards onto his cot.

"What are you, crazy?" he shouted. "Touching me like that with your filthy hands! It feels like somebody's thrown acid in my face!"

Hal was disconcerted.

"I just wanted to check," he explained.

"Why don't you feel your own?"

"I know that mine are real!"

Frank sat up suddenly. He lowered the hand he'd used to protect his smarting face. His half-closed eye glinted.

"What do you mean, real?"

"I had this idea that your cuts and gashes were phoney."

Frank shook his head.

"I don't get it."

"Like a disguise," said Hal, straightening up.

Frank leant over him.

"Come on, spit it out."

"It's hard to explain."

"Lost for words?"

Hal rose to the challenge implicit in the other man's question. Slowly he smoothed down his tousled hair.

"Well, thing is, the way I see it, it's a bit off, the two of us being put in the same cell."

"Ah!" said Frank. "Great minds think alike. I had the same idea."

Then they did what in the circumstances was the most unlikely thing: they smiled at each other.

In a level, almost friendly voice, Hal asked:

"Tell me... has somebody planted you here as a stool pigeon?"

"Nope," said Frank, without getting angry. "How about you?"

"I'm asking the question," said Hal. "That says it all..."

Frank thought about this. Then he gave a shrug.

"It doesn't say a damn thing! Or put it this way: it just means that you're trying to quiet my suspicions."

"All right, all right," sighed Hal as he stretched out on his bed again, "I can see your injuries are real... Cosh, was it?"

"Yeah... and fists... Cosh for the face and fists for the ribs... They know what they're doing."

"But what if they'd really done you over?" Hal went on after a moment's thought. "To make your cover look authentic."

Frank in turn lay face down on his cot.

"You must have some very important information to spill for me to be handed over to such high-class make-up artists."

"I've got nothing to spill," said Hal savagely.

"Me neither," said Frank. "So you see... we're quits!"

3

The night was long and filled with strange groans. The two men did not sleep. All through the interminable hours they lay, hands clasped behind their heads, gazing up at the dirt-encrusted blue night light and thought about their new situation.

Sometimes they jumped when their mute cellmate choked in his sleep or when the clammy silence was ripped apart by the nocturnal screams which are common enough in over-crowded places.

They did not exchange a word. From time to time they turned their heads towards each other and each caught the glitter of the whites of the other man's eyes. Then they would turn over onto their backs and stare up at the ceiling, which was too high and had a barred air vent set into it. Its opening looked like a foul, malevolent mouth which mocked their predicament.

At the far end of a secret universe an immense muffled roar pulsated—the ocean, which was close by. When dawn appeared through the bars of the vent, turning the night light pale, the two inmates sensed that the rumble of the waves would now die away. But in reality it was fatigue which dimmed the sounds around them. Both fell almost simultaneously into a trance-like slumber, which was not sleep but nevertheless transported them far from reality to a hazy zone that was iridescent and warm.

*

Shouts and the sound of measured footsteps dragged them out of their torpor.

The Bull ran his stick along the bars of their cell as though they were the strings of a harp.

"Time to shower!" he yelled.

He thrust his bloated face against the bars.

"Right, you new lads, settling down in our family boarding house, are you?"

He unlocked the cell door and left it ajar.

"Form up in lines! Hands behind your backs! And no talking, you dogs! Silence, or I'll rattle your bones with my rib-tickler!"

The mute was first out. He looked even more sallow here, under the corridor lights. His small rat's eyes, with their mealy eyelashes, kept flickering. The Bull helped him on his way with a kick, as he did every day.

He laughed out loud, proud of this miserable action, which he had brought to a pitch of perfection and wheeled out each morning with undiminished delight.

The mute scuttled to the end of the line of prisoners, all waiting in gloomy silence for the order to move.

Hal and Frank joined him.

"Forward, march!"

They moved off between an escort of armed warders. The shower room was located on the floor below.

It was basic. There were twenty or so cubicles with neither doors nor curtains in a row running along one wall. The facilities for washing consisted of a shower head and an on–off control in the form of a pull chain.

The prisoners undressed, hung their coarse canvas fatigues

on a row of pegs and showered while the warders looked on and kept up a flow of jeers at their expense.

Hal and Frank stripped to the skin with the rest of the men and stepped into adjacent cubicles. Through the steam filling the room, the prisoners were able to exchange a few words… Occasionally warders would bawl half-heartedly: "No talking!" The sound of splashing water was cheering and the punch of the warm water soothing.

Hal peeked over the top of the partition separating him from his new friend.

Frank spotted him.

"Peeping Tom are you?" he asked.

Hal gave a leering laugh and yanked the chain, which turned the water on. A stream of warm water rained down on his gleaming body.

"You're hardly marked about the body!" he called. "One bruise for effect, now that's a classy touch!… You took most of it on your mug, because that's where it shows most."

The water suddenly stopped flowing in the next cubicle and Frank was standing in front of him, shamelessly naked, with an angry crease on his forehead.

"You're not starting up on that same tack again, are you?"

Hal's eyes were flooded with water. He shook himself, released the shower chain and took one step forward.

"Not starting, continuing… If you think I'm going to be fooled by your sordid little game, you're making a big mistake!"

"What?"

They were wreathed in clouds of steam, and through the watery fog their movements were ghostly. Their bodies glistened like freshly caught fish.

"That's enough!" cried Frank as he advanced.

He slipped on the wet tiles and stumbled slightly forward. Hal assumed he was being attacked by his cellmate and threw a punch.

There was a damp thwack. Frank's face twisted with pain, for Hal's knuckles had landed on the cheek which had already been split open.

"Bastard!" he grunted. "You dirty swine!"

He launched himself. The thud of punches was lost in the coughing and spluttering of water in the pipes and the shouts of the warders.

Face to face, breathing hard, gasping for air, the two men slugged it out with silent fury in Hal's cubicle. They grunted briefly with pain when a punch struck home. Their eyes, irritated by the water, stood out from their heads.

"Goddammit! There's a couple of the bastards beating each other up here!" cried a voice.

Warders came at a run. Blows from batons rained down on the two prisoners from every angle and their anger evaporated abruptly.

The shower they'd already taken was followed by this other much more brutal kind.

"Animals!" roared the Bull. "Run these characters back to their cell! Take a hose to them! Hit them in the nuts! I'll drop in on them later and say hello."

Neither Hal nor Frank remembered how they'd managed to get dressed or how they'd got back to their cell at the junction of the two corridors. Everything happened in a bewildering frenzy. Hands grabbed them, feet kicked them, voices roared abuse in their ears, blood ran down their faces…

Then they were lying on their backs in the grey cell, and came round in a state of agonizing peace.

"That was a damn-fool stunt to pull!" said Hal.

"Don't give me that. You started it…"

Hal said nothing, his silence an admission of the truth of the charge.

Frank went on:

"Listen, pal, carry on like this and I'll knock your insinuations down your throat. Have you got that?"

"Only truth offends," murmured Hal.

Frank sat up.

"Say that again!"

"Oh, don't be a fool… Anyway, I don't give a damn whether you're a stoolie or not. All I'll say to you is that you're wasting your time."

But Hal was aching all over and utterly sick of it all.

"Same to you…" said Frank soberly. "You're wasting your time too… I can see through it, you know. You're taking this little game of yours too far…"

They both fell silent. The other inmates returned. They all craned their necks trying to get a glimpse of the two pugilists. The arrival of new prisoners always added excitement to their dull lives. They were curious about them.

When they'd all returned to their "home from home", the Bull walked into the cell on the heels of the mute. He locked the door behind him and nodded to one of the warders that he was to stay nearby. A happy little smile lit up his bloated face.

"It seems you are always ready for a scrap, then?" he asked in his high, thin voice.

He was chewing on a rose. The flower completely hid his mouth and his words seemed to come out of the red petals.

Neither man responded.

"Stand up when I'm talking to you!" he bawled at them. "I'm going to teach you respect!"

Hal and Frank got to their feet.

"Hands straight down the sides of your trousers!" thundered the chief warder. "Head straight, chin up a bit... Are you two catching my drift?"

The two prisoners did exactly what they were told but with such obvious bad grace that there was something insolent about their obedience.

The Bull unstrapped his leather stick and tapped the palm of his hand several times with it. He liked the sound it made. He especially liked sharing it with prisoners.

With amazing speed, he raised the supple baton and in a single sweep brought it down across both their faces.

The two men screamed simultaneously.

"That's right," said the fat man as he wiped beads of perspiration from his forehead. "Sing up, it chases away the blues... I warned you that house rules don't allow brawling. Next time I'll lay you out good and proper and you'll cop a week in solitary. We got everything here, boys! This is the last jail in France that still has cells with rats! Take my word for it! Rats as big as my thigh, are you listening?"

Both men gave a sign that they had heard.

"That was a word to the wise," added the Bull, who had a large collection of such ready-made sayings, as he left.

Frank turned to Hal.

The blow from the leather stick had left a savage mark on

Hal's face. It stretched across his cheeks like a bar, a purplish welt over which a bloody dew was slowly forming.

Frank looked away and sat on the edge of his cot. The mute pulled a dirty rag from underneath his pillow and held it for a moment under the tap. When the rag was soaked, he held it out to Hal.

Hal took it from their disabled cellmate with a brief nod of thanks. He sponged his face with it. The rag quickly turned red.

"For a guy who topped his wife," said Frank, "he's very considerate."

"It doesn't mean a man's got no feelings," said Hal. "Maybe she made his life hell. Women are good at that. From the moment you drag them off to the town hall they start behaving like pigs… That's the way it goes."

"You married?"

"For my sins…"

Hal gave the mute his rag back after rinsing it through.

"Thanks," he said, speaking clearly so that he would be understood.

The mute smiled sadly and slipped the rag back under his pillow.

"He was lucky, given the fix he was in," said Frank.

"Lucky?"

"Sure… Lucky to be in France… It's one of the few countries where you can do your missus in without having your head separated from your shoulders."

"A grand place right enough. The jails are comfortable… It's only the lack of sex that gets the thumbs-down."

He groaned. The cold water had temporarily dulled the pain but the whack he'd taken from from the leather stick

34

was now gnawing his cheeks with bared teeth… Fine, pointed teeth, closely set and sharp as a pike's.

"That guy," he murmured, "is a sadist."

"Damn right," said Frank. "They all get like that, more or less. Spending your life in jail without having to is a clue… How about you? Did you ever do time in prison?"

"This is my first stretch."

"Same here."

"So we've got one thing in common," said Hal. "What did you do on the outside?"

"I sold petrol," said Frank after a moment.

"You mean you were a pump attendant?"

"No, traveller for an oil company."

"That's something else we got in common," said Hal happily. "You sold petrol and I used it. I drove trucks."

"Do you like strawberries?" Frank asked unexpectedly.

His cellmate looked at him, wondering if he was trying to get a rise out of him. But Frank seemed to be serious.

"Yes," he answered. "Why are you asking?"

Frank got up and approached Hal's cot. He bent his knees and leant them on the wooden frame.

"So do I, Hal," he said, without ceasing to be deadly serious, "so do I. I like strawberries too. So you see, that makes a third thing we've got in common. Keep on looking and we might find more. Look, what's the idea? You want me to be like you, or you to be like me? Or maybe your old man canoodled with my old lady or my old dad with your ma? Or maybe we could be brothers?…"

He grabbed Hal by the lapels of his fatigues.

"Would that make you happy?"

Hal firmly pushed him off.

"You're a clown!" he muttered.

"And you're not, I suppose? Watch your step, pal, or you'll get into what makes us different and that would be a real shame!"

He stood up, did a few physical jerks, then walked to the far wall and leant against it just under the small high window. The sun did not shine into their narrow cell because a wall nearby was in its way. But the aperture allowed a square patch of bluey-green light to enter. By now, the muffled roar of the sea had melted into the background noise of the prison... At times the despairing cries of seabirds drifted in, raucous and plaintive.

"Trying for a tan?" asked Hal after staring at his companion upside down.

"In a sense, yes," said Frank.

"What sense is that?" growled Hal.

"The other sense... I mean the wider sense... The sun... Do you think the sun still exists?"

"I don't know," sighed Hal. "I don't know anything any more!"

4

But the sun was still there. They were able to deduce as much that afternoon during exercise.

They were only able to get a sense of its presence from between four grey cliffs enclosing the yard. The exercise hour never coincided with the moment when the sun was directly above the bleak cement rectangle. Cement! Bars! Greyness!...

The men walked round and round in a circle with their hands held behind their backs. In the middle of the yard, a warder sat on a stool, on which he swivelled as and when he needed to.

"He's going to give himself the staggers," a prisoner whispered in Frank's ear.

Frank gave an imperceptible nod.

Encouraged, the prisoner went on:

"That was one hell of a scrap between you and your pal. How come the pair of you went at it hammer and tongs in the shower?"

Frank looked up and said out of the corner of his mouth:

"Incompatible temperaments..."

"Like a divorce case," sniggered the man.

The warder bawled:

"Halt!"

The joyless procession stopped.

"Oi, Mariole!" called the warder.

The prisoner who had just spoken to Frank stepped out of the line and started walking towards the warder.

"You called me, Monsieur Plaud?"

"Were you chatting with the new man?" asked the warder.

He was red-haired, young and wearing glasses. He looked like a school prefect. He had that same nasty look in his eye and the same power complex.

"Course not, Monsieur Plaud."

"Shut up! And don't lie. I saw you."

Prisoner Mariole smiled obsequiously.

"Since you saw me, Monsieur Plaud, I can't deny it. You don't miss a trick. Sometimes I wonder if you don't have eyes in the back of your head…"

"Button your lip!" said the warder.

Still, he was flattered by the prisoner's comment about his keen eyesight.

"What were you saying to that smart chancer?"

"That he'd been stupid to mix it with the other one."

"Yeah…" said the warder. "They're both idiots, but they won't do it again!" He yelled: "Am I right, you two?"

Frank and Hal nodded their heads:

"Oh no, sir, it won't happen again, sir!"

It happened again the same day. But this time, it all went badly wrong for them.

After the evening meal, the three of them were in the same cell watching the daylight fade in the small high window. Suddenly Frank asked Hal, point-blank:

"What was it you did that landed you in here?"

Hal did not answer at once, as if he hadn't heard the question. At length, just as Frank had stopped expecting to get an answer, he murmured:

"Oh, just stuff…"

"What stuff?" Frank persisted.

"What about you?"

"You've got a funny way of answering questions…"

There was a lengthy silence. The night light came on. It cast a bluish glow over the wall, which grew stronger as the daylight died.

Frank turned on his side.

"It was night…" he said.

Hal knew straight away that though nothing had led up to it, Frank was beginning to tell his story.

"I was in a town up north…"

He stopped, distracted by the variety and flow of his memories.

"Go on," said Hal. "You're getting me interested."

Frank obliged and continued:

"I'd called on my clients during the day and decided to spend the night in a small inn… But they didn't have garage space for my car… I had to park the jalopy in a farmyard…"

"What happened?" asked Hal in a voice from which he stripped any suggestion of curiosity, to avoid giving Frank the satisfaction of making him wait.

But Frank was not fooled:

"Are you really interested?" he asked.

"Course I am!"

"When I got to the farmyard, the wife was watering the horses… She was carrying a storm lantern."

"I can see it now," mused Hal.

"She was short and fat and wore a headscarf."

"What happened then?"

This time, Hal could not disguise his curiosity.

"Get lost!" Frank snarled suddenly.

"Oh, suit yourself… No need to get stroppy!"

Hal sighed and groped his way to the tap. He turned it on and splashed water on his face. Then he drank from the tap. The water was warm and tasted of copper.

"She had large, flabby breasts," Frank resumed.

Hal smiled in the dark and sat on the foot of his bed, facing the storyteller. There was less than a metre between them.

"Hell!" he smiled. "You're starting to strike me as a bit of a skirt-lifter in your own small way… Large, flabby breasts, eh?"

Frank shrugged his shoulders.

"Everyone can have a moment of madness… at certain times."

"True," said Hal.

"Sometimes it goes wrong. Other times, it turns out all right…"

"Did it go wrong for you?"

"You see…"

"Did you rape the farmer's wife?"

"Shut your mouth!" cried Frank. "I don't like that word," he added, lowering his voice. "I grabbed her… She started shaking… Then screaming… I tipped her into the straw—the yard was full of it… I had her… with the flames blazing round us…"

"Flames!" cried Hal. "What flames?"

"The lamp had tipped over onto the straw."

Hal pictured the scene. A frown suddenly spread over his face and he said in a quiet voice: "Surrounded by flames! Damn! I'd have paid good money to get an eyeful of that. What happened then?"

"I panicked."

"And?…"

Frank reached with both hands in the gloom. His hands were big and covered with fair hair. Hal stared at them the way people stare at objects displayed in a glass case.

"You strangled her?"

"Yes," Frank said without elaborating. "Right, your turn now… Let's have it."

Hal stretched out on his mattress, which creaked under him.

"Oh with me, it was simpler. It happened in a truck drivers' cafe… I was a bit pie-eyed. I got into a shouting match with this guy who was there. It was about politics. I'm not interested in politics—it's so damned stupid! All it's good for is making a small number of crooked characters very rich."

"What happened?" Frank broke in.

"Oh yes… What can I say? I didn't like the line the guy was shooting. So I smashed a beer bottle over his skull, but it turned out his skull was pretty thin!"

"What kind?" Frank asked matter-of-factly.

It took Hal a moment or two for the question to register. "What?" he said.

"The beer," Frank explained. "What kind of beer was it?"

"Virginia."

"Are you sure?"

Hal became suspicious.

"Of course. When I raised the bottle I saw the label upside down… It's the sort of thing you remember!"

"You're lying!" cried Frank, leaping to his feet.

"I swear…"

"And I swear you're lying through your teeth! Virginia bottles don't have necks. So you couldn't have crowned anybody with one."

Hal went quiet. He opened his mouth to protest but changed his mind.

"You never thought of that, did you, you dummy!" Frank said as he kicked the mattress his cellmate was lying on. "Bull! Pure bull! Anybody would think you were trying to pull the wool over my eyes…"

The mute sat up in his cot when he saw that the two men were at each other's throats. He looked at each in turn, uncomprehending. He didn't dare intervene…

Frank grabbed Hal round the neck.

"What do you want from me, eh? What are you after?"

Hal bucked, straightened his back and managed to get hold of his attacker's wrists.

He was unusually strong. Frank released his grip. When he had been forced back, Hal growled:

"Listen, Frank. A man's entitled to spin himself whatever yarn he likes, isn't he? Anyway, you started it…"

"What do you mean?"

"That farmer's wife with her flabby breasts and her storm lantern and the guy jumping into the middle of an inferno! You read that in James Hadley Chase!"

Frank looked down. Hal let go of his wrists and his arms dropped loosely down the sides of his body, where they hung like two broken branches.

"You wanted to wrong-foot me, didn't you, you bastard," barked Hal. "Don't you think I got your number the first time I set eyes on you? Your face gives you away—it says what you are trying to hide. It's got *stoolie* written all over it! It's as obvious as if it was up there in lights!"

"Are you going to shut your mouth?" bawled Frank.

He was jumping up and down with rage. His whole body was shaking. His teeth chattered with fury.

"I said shut your trap!"

"Stoolie!" yelped Hal. "Stoolie!"

He flung the insult as though it were a complaint. It was almost a cry of anguish. He put his whole being into it... His whole life...

"Stoolie!"

The word rose through the silence of the sleeping prison. As it travelled it woke the others from their dreams. Protesting voices from every side blended into a chorus:

"What's going on?"

"It's those new men kicking up a rumpus!"

"Move them to another cell!"

"Knock it off, will you!"

The sound of footsteps... The screws were coming, and they were not in the best of moods...

Frank had got Hal by the throat again.

"You're the stoolie! It's you!"

"That's right," grunted Hal gasping for breath. "I got my face smashed in so I could come and listen to you tell boring stories. Your plan's a bit obvious, you know. Spreading lies so you can get to the truth..."

Frank let him go. He'd suddenly had an idea. He said:

"Show me your hands!"

"But..."

"Come on, show me your hands!"

Hal held out his hands in the glow of the night light. Frank spat on them.

"Call those truck driver's hands?" he said calmly. "Who do you think you're kidding? You were still having manicures the day before yesterday!"

"And what about you, a travelling rep for an oil company!... Tell me, Monsieur Shell: where exactly were you prospecting?"

"Pas-de-Calais," said Frank with a scowl.

"Right! So what's the name of the guy who's got the contract in Saint-Omer? Well?"

Frank gave a shrug.

"Just drop it," he murmured.

"That's more like it!" gloated Hal. "You see, it's you!... You're just a low-down cop!"

"Say that again!"

"A lower-than-a-rat's-tail cop!"

They laid into each other once more, rolling around, grappling on the floor. They were still at it when the warders separated them using boots and cudgels.

When the Bull showed up, in his slippers, all that remained for him to do was administer the final touches with his stick to the pair, who were now incapable of reacting in any way.

"Take these two lowlifes down to solitary," he ordered. "Each man in a cell of his own! And put them both on bread and water! And don't forget to go gentle on them: they're delicate little things!"

But they did not wear kid gloves, and the two prisoners were bundled roughly down to the floors below.

As they passed, their fellow prisoners, whose sleep they had disrupted, hurled abuse at them.

Before he left, the Bull swatted the mute with his stick.

The man with no voice cowered on his bed and began to weep for a world full of sorrows.

When he said that there were rats in the solitary cells, the Bull had not overstated the facts. The arrival of a new prisoner in the windowless basement dungeons was always manna from heaven for the rodents, because with him came loaves of bread, which the newcomer had to fight for with the repulsive sitting tenants…

5

A week went by in those two tomb-like dungeons. A week, as slow and black as the blackest night. When the two men emerged they were taken straight to the prison governor, a tall, acerbic man who read them the standard lecture on good behaviour, which ended:

"I could separate you, of course, but that would be the easy answer. I prefer to think that you will reach some form of gentleman's agreement… if I can put it that way," he added, with a look full of contempt.

"Now get out. Any more antics from you and I promise that I'll come down on you like a ton of bricks."

Frank and Hal had not looked at each other since they had been reunited. They were marched out of the governor's office, eyes furiously to the front so that they would not have to acknowledge each other's existence until the very last moment.

The Bull, who was boss on their floor, was waiting for them. There was a rose between his teeth, which would have looked more at home on a sick horse.

"Why, if it isn't my old pals!" he said. "Well, I did tell you that I'd be keeping an eye on the two of you… From now on, you play by the rules… I like lads who stay in step…"

He had followed them into their cell and sat down next to the mute, who looked scared to death.

"Now see here," he said, giving a sigh of contentment, "if you go on larruping each other like this, you'll very likely end up dead… Whichever of you puts the other one's lights out for good will automatically be for Charlie Chop... Never heard of it? It's an amazing thing... The guy who invented it was called Guillotin... And he was a doctor!... As you see, I know my French history!"

He gave a blood-curdling laugh.

"A public benefactor... A machine for cutting troublemakers down to size... It's already paid us three visits since I've been here!... We have to get up early, but there's a bit more money in it for us... And it's coming again, boys... in just a couple of weeks... We've got a customer needs a haircut. A citizen who mowed down two cops—not a wise move, you could say... Such a reckless lad!

"The poor lamebrain has these fantastic notions! He imagines the president is going to give him a pardon! It'll never happen! Police hides are sacred!"

He talked to get himself high on power, on crude words and graphic images.

At length he stood up, and with the short steps of a fat man shuffled to the door.

"I want it nice and qui-et," he said. "Do you understand?"

He slammed the door behind him. The key turned in the lock.

"Hi there," said Hal. "How was the holiday?"

"Had a great time, thanks."

Frank eyed his companion.

"My word," he said, "you must have been by the sea—you look a picture of health."

"You don't say."

"I do, yes. Seems to me your spell in the hole was never going to put you on the sick list. The truth is it was all a fit-up

47

to give you a breather. You were starting to have enough of it here, weren't you?"

Hal faced up to Frank.

"You're not going to start up on that again, are you?" said Hal sadly.

The sad note surprised Frank.

"Look at the daylight," said Hal.

"What are you up to now?"

He turned his head mechanically towards where Hal had pointed: the high window.

"Your eyes are normal," muttered Hal.

"What do you mean, normal?"

"Are they normal?"

"What would you expect them to be? Crossed?"

"No, sensitive to light. When you've been in a black slammer for a week, your peepers get used to the dark. And afterwards... Here, have a look at mine..."

He turned and faced the light. His eyes blinked. The brightness made them water.

"You keep coming up with these dopey ideas!" sighed Frank as he stretched out on his bed. "Oh yes, Hal, I was in the slammer, all right!... With those stinking rats..."

He held up his right foot. A slice of the sole of the sandal was missing and the braided rope was frayed.

"They even tried to eat me! I really thought I'd leave my hide in that devil's hellhole!"

Hal stared at the rope-soled sandal and nodded.

"Right," he said. "I see... You'd think we'd been transported back a century... Cells full of rats! Now isn't that something? And here we are, in the middle of the twentieth century!"

48

"Oh, you and your centuries," said Frank.

"It's the same with the way the screws beat us up… I'm not kidding!"

"Get away! There have always been men who beat up other men and there always will be… Anyway, seeing screws beat up prisoners is no worse than seeing prisoners trying to brain each other at every opportunity!"

Hal did not respond.

"What?"

"Don't you think so?" persisted Frank.

"Sure," said Hal. "That's what I think. And I even wonder…"

"…what I think about you, right?… Maybe I've got you all wrong…"

Frank watched the slow progress of a cockroach over the wall. It scuttled across a bare patch at high speed. Then suddenly it swooped down onto Dumbo's mattress.

"That's something else that I'm wondering," Frank admitted. "We got this idea into our heads from day one… And now it's grown into some sort of disease that's spreading and eating us up!"

He knelt down next to Hal's cot and asked in a crushed voice:

"Tell me, Hal: you're not a cop, are you?"

"Of course not," said Hal. "Because the cop here is you!"

Frank whined: "Not again! You just said…"

"Fair enough… I'm sorry."

"Even if I was one…" stammered Frank. "Let's have this out, Hal… Even if I was a cop… Even if I was… maybe we could still get on, since we have to put up with the same hardships and the same humiliations."

"You're right," agreed Hal. "Listen, let's go through the motions: let's shake hands!"

They looked each other in the eye for some time. They weren't sure, still fighting with a last glimmer of hate and also against the fear of looking ridiculous. Then their fingers touched and they shook hands.

"Even if you are a cop, Hal," muttered Frank.

"Even if you're one," sighed Hal.

6

The Bull was the first to notice that an alteration had come about in the relations between the two men. He was a limited, rough sort of man, but he was streetwise, and that made up for what he lacked in intelligence. Fifteen years of service in a prison had taught him the rudiments of psychology, which enabled him to follow the changing states of mind of his "customers".

"Hey, you two!" he exclaimed on the day following the "declaration of peace" signed by Hal and Frank. "You're both behaving as if you're as pally as pigs in muck. Only goes to show that my method works! Rules are like music: you apply the first with a rod and strike up the second with a baton!"

The most unpleasant thing about this man was the soapy laugh which punctuated his witticisms. It stung, it sidled into you like a woodlouse and defiled something you couldn't put a name to.

"Only a fortnight now before the execution…" the fat man said, as if he were talking to himself. "Anyway, it'll make a nice change… And I'll tell you the best bit: the formal rites will be taking place on the same day as the local fete and gala in town. On our programme: Losing your Head… Short Back and Sides… The Flashing Blade… Parade with Band… Merry-go-round and Grand Ball. Have you noticed how balls on posters are always 'grand'?"

He laughed more uproariously than usual. It was a laugh which started in his belly and climbed up his entire body in concentric quakings.

He winked.

"Charlie Chop!…" he guffawed. "A real treat for the tender-hearted… Some invention, eh? And such drama!"

He left abruptly as he always did. He would talk and talk and then suddenly drop the subject and cancel the rest of his lecture.

"Bull!" grunted Hal. "The name suits him to a T!"

Frank shook his head.

"You've got to try to understand him," he said. "But he said it himself: he don't get many nice changes! But tell me, Hal, people who go to a circus to see the human cannonball, why do they do it? They fork out 500 francs for the dubious hope of seeing a man get himself killed, that's why! In here, there's no charge and there's never any doubt about the result, so you can imagine…"

"In *here*," sighed Hal. "The word's like a splinter I've got stuck in my finger… Here! In here!"

"Too damn right," agreed Frank. "And that's more than enough pain to be going on with, thank you very much!"

"Every time I say it or think of the words, the other ones come into my mind too."

"The other what?"

"The other words, the ones that mean the opposite: out there! Right?"

"Out there!" murmured Frank dreamily.

"Yes!" said Hal, his eyes ablaze. "Out there! Where there's air and plants and animals!… People piling into cinemas or going home to make love! Don't you ever think about that, about two people getting it on with each other? A bed! A woman, with the salt taste of her mouth… the smell of her!…"

Frank leapt off his cot and grabbed the bars of his cell with both hands.

"Stop it," he said dully. "Keep your trap shut! You're not doing us any favours! When you're rotting in a jail like this, you shouldn't talk about such stuff."

"You're right," agreed Hal. "Rotting's the word... damn right it is! And this is just the start of it. There'll be days and days..."

"Years, Hal!"

"Worse: hours. It's the hours that get you down the most."

Frank held his face so hard against the bars that they left white marks on his cheeks.

"I've had a bellyful of it," he said.

He'd spoken matter-of-factly, without raising his voice. It was an admission, an admission of infinitely human frailty.

"Never mind," murmured Hal. "Maybe we'll get used to it..."

"You wish! You can't get used to something you can't take any more! You can't get used to this greyness everywhere, to the walls, to the hours which never stop dripping onto our heads, one after another... Take the guy in the condemned cell waiting for the executioner to come for him... At least he can concentrate on one specific thing... He still has hope, a wonderful hope: he's hoping that he'll live... But me..."

He let himself slide down onto the floor until he was sitting on his heels. He rested his head on his knees.

"I'm alone, with a past which is dying inside me like some plant that nobody waters any more!"

After a moment, he looked up. There was a hard gleam in his eyes and his jaw was slack.

"I tell you, Hal. I'd gladly swap places with that guy..."

"What guy, Frank?"

"The one they're going to shorten... Dying's as good as a rest, right?... One jolt and it's 'Good night all!' The earth drops away under you, like you're a red balloon and someone has let go of the string."

Hal shook his head.

"Wonder of wonders!" he said. "Infinity on every floor!"

"Hal!" cried Frank in a voice full of anguish.

"Yes?"

"What if you're not a cop after all?"

"Oh, not that again! No one knows better than you that if there's a cop here, it's not me!"

But Frank took no notice.

"Hal, we could try something..."

"What do you have in mind?" asked Hal.

"Don't you see?"

They stared at each other. Hal got up, and went and looked out through the bars. Lowering his voice, he said:

"I can see very well... And if I didn't think you really were a—"

"Leave it!"

"...I'd have suggested it long ago."

"Do you think it's possible?"

"No!"

"Look, I really need to try something impossible."

"Me too," said Hal. "Do you reckon there've been guys who've escaped from here?"

"I don't even want to think about it. Other guys don't matter!"

They both lay face down on their cots and remained for some time without speaking. The idea which had just hatched in their heads was enough to occupy their minds. They closed their eyes, oblivious to the presence of their dumb cellmate, whose hole-in-the-corner existence did not interfere with their thoughts. The distant roar of the sea did not trouble them either. They were lost in their fanciful dreams and nothing mattered to them except their wild scheme.

"We'll be running a big risk," said Hal.

"Getting hit by bullets as we get away… or hunted down by dogs… or by men!… Any one of them would be painful… But, the hell with it, why should that bother us?"

"Right!" said Hal. "Too damn right!"

Then they returned to their idle musings. Suddenly, Hal exclaimed:

"I got an idea!"

"What idea?"

"At least for the date of… of the caper!"

"Caper's the word for it!"

"We do it on the day they execute that guy…"

"Why?"

Hal beamed, looking very pleased with himself.

"Try this for size, man. The Bull said the execution is going to be held on some local holiday. From early morning there'll be a lot of coming and going in this place, right? Since it's a pretty depressing sight, the screws will be trying to keep their spirits up. The ones that are off duty will be out making the most of the fair, the rest will have a drink or two… In other words, the routine will be different: are you with me?"

Frank nodded.

"Yes, that's pretty smart thinking. And now I'm going to tell you who is going to open the cell door for us."

"Who?"

"The Bull," said Frank mysteriously.

"Have you included miracles in our marriage settlement?"
Frank shook his head.

"It's no miracle, Hal. Have you noticed how he likes dropping
in here for a chat? He's fond of the sound of his own voice...
We'll keep an eye out for him... When he comes anywhere near,
we'll pretend we're having an argument. He'll be in here like a
flash! You can count on him. And once he's here..."

"We jump him!" Hal said callously.

"We'll punch his lights out permanent!"

"That's what I mean by jumping him!"

"We'll take his keys!" said Frank.

"Yes... and his piece!"

They continued discussing their plan for the rest of that
day and, when night came, they were still sitting side by side
on the same bed, whispering vague thoughts to each other.

They were still there when the Bull took them by surprise.
His pasty face appeared suddenly through the bars.

"Aha!... Still chatting, are we, in this neck of the woods?
No, no, Nanette! You'll have to button it, boys! It's time! The
time when the imagination does what the temperature of the
sick does: it rises! It's like the air is full of girls! It's not good for
the health! So you'd best lie on your bellies and think about
something else!... Something depressing. Like life, for example!"

He broke off to spit the flower he was chewing into the
middle of the cell, as was his wont.

"Myself, I'm off to my bed. My old lady's already there,
ready and waiting. Oh, if you only knew my Suzanne! A pair
of buttocks on her like a mare!"

He gave a chortle of delight.

Hal cleared his throat. He was about to come out with something insulting, but Frank squeezed his arm hard to shut him up.

"Did you want to say something?" asked the Bull in his sugary voice, for he hadn't missed Hal's reaction.

Hal shook his head.

"Nothing, chief!"

"Good… I like men who can keep their mouths sewn up! Right, I'll say goodnight, then!"

The scuffing sound of shoes and he was gone.

"See?" said Hal. "Perhaps the thing I like best about our plan is that it starts with that bastard getting bumped off!"

He picked up the faded rose the big man had spat out.

"Since he likes flowers, we'll make sure that's what he's going to get," he murmured.

PART II

Beauty

7

The two weeks that followed were almost as happy as the time leading up to the day when people go off on holiday.

Making plans for their escape generated a kind of infectious high spirits. Instead of being apprehensive, tense and on edge, Hal and Frank felt agreeably excited. It was good that the thing had been decided.

They were now swept up on the wings of bright hopes. Of course, it would end with a death, but that hardly mattered. After all, wasn't the most important thing to stay focused on an idea? They had grabbed it as they would a battering ram—and in fact their idea was itself a battering ram, with which they would try to smash down the gates...

For example, the night before the eagerly awaited fourteenth day, neither of them could sleep. They were restless and kept their ears open. There were vague noises in the prison, noises that were very sinister when the mind imagined what they might be.

The death cells were located at the other end of the building. But when night began to turn grey, the comings and goings in that part of the prison could be clearly heard by the two prisoners.

They got up at frequent intervals for a drink of water. At a given moment, not far away, a man who was soon to die was being woken up.

They did not speak. Seeing them stir, the mute sat up in his cot and looked at them questioningly.

Frank raised the side of one hand to his throat and with the other gestured vaguely towards a point beyond the walls. The mute understood and his eyes clouded with sudden fear.

Hal splashed water on his face to wake himself up.

"The lousiest part of it," he said, "is that they turf the guy out of bed so they can chop his head off. Why don't they do it in the afternoon?... Or better, why not the evening?... When everybody's had it all up to here?... Seems to me it wouldn't be such a big deal..."

"Too right," murmured Frank. "But it would stop the lawyers droning on and on!"

Just before the "great moment" arrived, the prison shook with the noise made by prisoners as they rapped on the pipes to give the news: *Pardon refused! Poligny for the chop!*

Uproar raged throughout the building. Prisoners gave each other a leg-up so that they could reach the high window in their cells.

Since the windows were angled upwards they could see nothing of what went on in the courtyard. But at least they could hurl abuse into the cold dawn air and they made the most of the opportunity.

"Come on, Poligny! Death to cops!"

Hal and Frank listened intently.

"Think the guy can hear?" asked Hal.

"I don't know. He must be deaf if he can't, no?"

"Absolutely."

Eventually calm was restored and the prison settled back into its usual state of torpor. But there was still a sense of unease in the air. Something had happened. Something ugly.

Several hours went by. Snatches of music were heard. The fun of the fair was starting.

"Maybe we could make a start with our own party," said Frank.

"Agreed."

"Any regrets?"

"You don't have regrets in advance. Regrets, as the word suggests—"

"That's enough of your evening classes," growled Frank. "This isn't the time. Now, have you got everything clear?"

"Everything."

Even so, Frank went over it again:

"We start yelling at each other the minute we spot the Bull. He walks in…"

"We hope…"

"He'll come in all right."

"If you say so…"

"Then I grab his hands and you get him round the neck to stop him yelling his head off…"

"Got it…"

"And squeeze hard—give it all you've got!"

"Trust me, man!"

They were both pale-faced and avoided looking each other in the eye.

They stood up and walked in circles a few times to stretch their legs. They swung their arms too…

"What next?" murmured Hal. He went on: "Yes, I know, the keys and the gun… But after that, Frank, what do we do then?"

Frank gave a weary shrug.

"What do you want me to say?… We go to the end of the corridor—at least we hope so. There's a big iron door. We open it with the keys. On the far side is the screws' surveillance post. I hope there's not too many of them there and that they won't put up a fight because I shoot fast…"

"Hold it!" Hal broke in. "You say you're quick on the draw. Does that mean you're assuming you'll have the gun?"

"Like I said, I shoot fast and don't miss!"

"So do I, Frank. I can shoot fast and straight too."

"On a good day I can drill the ace of hearts out of a playing card at fifteen paces!"

"And on a bad day I can drill a man though the heart at twenty! That's as good, isn't it?"

Frank burst out laughing.

"Just listen to us!" he said. "Our little outing has got off to a good start! We're already arguing about the gun!"

"We're not arguing," said Hal. "I'm only saying I've got as much right to have the gun as you!"

"OK, let's toss for it."

Hal wrenched a button off his fatigues.

"If you guess which hand the button's in," he said, "you get the piece."

"Agreed."

Frank screwed up his eyes and stared at the two clenched fists which were being held out to him. He hesitated.

"Right," he said after a while.

Hal opened his left hand and revealed the button.

"That's it, then," said Frank stoically. "All square and above board."

"Don't worry, I won't let you down."

Hal flexed his fingers as if they were already gripping the steel butt of a gun.

"Listen, when we burst in on the screws I'll shout: 'Get your hands up!' Right?"

"Wrong!" Frank said. "It's only in films that they do it that way. Remember, a man who shouts makes less of an impression than a man who doesn't say anything. Wave the gun in their faces and they'll get the message without any need to draw a picture..."

"Right... And then what do we do?"

"If they don't make any trouble I'll get their guns... That'll give us firepower in reserve. You can't have too many shooters when you go AWOL..."

"And what if they do make trouble?"

"You say you're quick on the draw?"

"But after that... What happens after?"

"Well, we'll see. I'll unlock the door to the courtyard. We'll be through it like a bat out of hell. We'll still have a fair stretch of open ground to cover. The machine gun on the watchtower will open up. We'll have to keep ducking and weaving..."

"Not me!" Hal growled. "I'm going in a straight line. Oh yes! I'm a guy in a hurry..."

"Suit yourself... So, assuming we make it to the main exit, we'll try to talk down the guard on the gate. If that doesn't work at least we'll have had a sniff of fresh air..."

Suddenly, Hal, who had been going round in circles, stopped in front of the barred door.

His companion joined him. He'd understood. The Bull was walking along the main stem of the T. He was alone.

Without wasting a moment, Frank grabbed Hal to him and gave him a deafening slap across the face.

"Take that, you swine!" he cried.

The blow spurred Hal to action. He threw himself wildly into battle slinging wild punches at his companion in earnest, and cursing at the top of his voice...

The Bull came at a run, drawn by the disturbance. But contrary to expectations, he did not enter the cell but stayed outside, content to watch the fight through the bars.

Both opponents, who kept watching him out of the corner of their eyes, almost had their hearts in their mouths. They suddenly stopped hitting each other and, breathing hard, turned towards the Bull.

"Seems like you just put the rematch off till now," the chief warder said smoothly.

"Is he going to make up his mind to come in?" the two cellmates wondered anxiously.

Hal had a brainwave.

"You got to excuse us, boss... We..."

He backed away as if the Bull were about to come in and he were afraid he'd get beaten up. The ploy galvanized the Bull. He wanted part of this action. With a practised gesture he unlocked the door. His small, pig-like eyes were bloodshot.

"No!..." pleaded Hal. "Please don't!... We... we won't do it again, boss..."

The fat man's stick whistled as he waved it in the air. He bore down on Hal, who flattened himself against the wall, ready to strike. Quick as a dog, Frank sprang. The Bull gave a short grunt and went down. Then Hal piled in and his strong hands closed around the chief screw's neck. But it's not easy to strangle a large man with bare hands.

Still struggling, the Bull succeeded in crying out. Seeing the danger, Frank began to sing. Now, sometimes a prisoner started singing a song which the others then picked up and joined in with all together. As a general rule, the screws never interfered. They knew that men need to shout and yell. So it was better that they got it off their chest by singing.

"Down at La Bastille, Nini Dog-skin's the girl for us…"

Other voices took it up:

"She's so cute and she's so sweet…"

As he sang, he went on putting his boot into the chief warder's belly while Hal gritted his teeth and squeezed the throat of his victim like a madman.

Suddenly, their mute cellmate realized what was happening. He'd been asleep and a kick from the Bull's boot had rattled the side of his bed and woken him up. He threw himself between his two companions and tried to separate them.

"Stupid bastard, poking his nose in!…" Hal said savagely.

He released the Bull's throat and using both hands punched the mute who staggered backwards onto his cot. Then, to settle the hash of the chief warder, who was still squealing like a wounded horse, he yanked the latter's revolver from its leather holster and started hitting him over the head with the butt. The large man went slack. His mouth opened and he gave a solemn sigh. Frank stopped singing. Sweat was pouring down his face. All the prisoners on their floor were now giving Aristide Bruant's ditty all they had:

"She's so cute and she's so sweet… the girl for us… Nini Dog-skin… Down at La Bastiiiille…"

"Quick!" said Hal. "Have you got the keys?"

"Here they are."

"So let's go, man! Chop chop!…"

They quickly stepped out into the corridor. There were no screws in sight. Suddenly the singing stopped because the prisoners had just realized what was going on. Faces, hands gripping bars—it was the same as the day they'd been brought in.

Then voices starting shouting excitedly:

"Come on, boys! You're not going without us? Quick! Open this door! Hurry up! Let us out!"

But Hal and Frank did not listen. They were half out of their minds. They felt as if they were naked in the middle of a crowd... Or that they were crossing a river on a tightrope.

They ran to the end of the corridor... The iron door opened just as they reached it and two warders came through saying:

"What the hell is..."

Hal showed them the gun. One of them put his hands up. The other reached for his holster. There was a dry *crack!* Hal had fired. The warder went down. Frank head-butted the other man savagely in the chest.

"Come on!" he cried. "Move it!"

They went through the door and came out inside the surveillance post. There was only one screw there. He had his hand on the internal phone.

"Leave it!" barked Hal.

The man obeyed.

Frank passed behind him and took his revolver. Then he poked the barrel into the defenceless man's broad back and pulled the trigger five times. There was an exalted look on his face that sent a shiver down Hal's spine.

8

The man who could not speak sat up and rubbed his skull. His head was spinning. He staggered out of his cell and stared uncomprehendingly at the dozens of hands which were being brandished through the bars on both sides of the corridor. At the far end of the central walkway two men were lying on the floor... One was starting to get up but the other was dead. A large red pool was spreading under him.

The mute walked through the double row of waving hands. Behind the hands were faces, wild faces, with mouths which kept opening. He did not understand. To him, there was only silence, as usual—cold, frightening silence. It was all beyond him; it was happening in another world, from which he was separated by a wall of thick glass.

The uninjured warder drew his revolver and waved it at him. The deaf mute continued to advance. He also saw the warder's mouth open but he did not understand the words at all. There was a burst of flame at the end of the barrel and he suddenly felt as if a warm sheet had been thrown over him, enveloping him completely... It was a good feeling. A wave of weakness took his legs from beneath him. He fell on his knees. Above him, the forest of hands continued to flap in the air. His head whirled... He fell at an angle across the corridor and died understanding nothing.

A hail of bullets raised a cloud of dust under Hal's feet. He looked at Frank, who was high-tailing it in front of him. Another two metres and they would be out of sight of the machine gun, for the prison gate was recessed into the wall.

He put on a tremendous spurt, kicking hard to overcome his own weight. Then they'd made it! At least for the moment. Gasping for breath he leant against the gate and looked around. Nothing moved in the courtyard. All there was in the whole world was the chatter of the machine gun, which went on firing blind, and the wail of the siren that sounded the alarm.

The duty guard was standing at the door of the gatehouse. He'd seen them coming and one absurd detail turned the drama of the scene into farce: he couldn't get his gun out of his holster. The mechanism which held the cover shut had jammed and the little sliding catch would not budge. The man's panic was doubtless partly responsible.

"Come on, come on!" snarled Frank. "Pull your finger out and open up!"

The guard abandoned his uncooperative holster. He made a jittery movement as if one of his senior officers had been watching him.

"Move it!" growled Hal. "If this gate isn't open in ten seconds, you're dead meat!..."

The man unhooked a massive key from his belt.

The wail of the siren and the rattle of the machine gun had cut the festivities short. Or, more accurately, they had scattered the festive crowd. The wide esplanade which ran from the prison down to the port was deserted when the two fugitives emerged onto it.

To encourage the travelling-show people to return to their caravans and discourage heroics, Frank loosed off a shot in the general direction of the now petrified fairground. A merry-go-round went on turning to the sound of faltering music... His bullet ended up in a lottery wheel, which was sent spinning. It made an eerie whirring noise.

"What number did you put your money on?" asked Hal with a laugh.

But it wasn't really a laugh, more a savage bark. Freedom had unnerved him.

He led the way at a run, his head well down as if he were expecting to get hit by a bullet. But the machine gun suddenly stopped firing. The guard manning it must have just realized the pointlessness of shooing at nothing.

Hal took a quick look back over his shoulder.

"Here they come!" he cried. "Get going!..."

Uniformed guards were emerging at the top of the esplanade.

If it hadn't been for the travelling fair, the two escaped prisoners would not have got ten paces across the space, which offered no cover. They would have been mown down as surely as if they had been facing a firing squad. But the rides and stands through which they sprinted acted as a series of providential screens.

They came out onto the quayside of the small port, where a few pleasure boats bobbed up and down next to the fishing vessels.

Frank spotted a small motorboat. It was like a floating spar to a drowning man—unless, that is, its engine were seized up. He took a quick look behind him. Everything seemed normal.

He jumped nimbly into it.

Hal followed him. The boat rocked.

"Any idea of how we can get this thing going?" asked Hal as he held his sides trying to catch his breath.

"Leave it to me. I've driven one of these before."

Frank was calmer than his companion. His hands were not shaking and Hal felt something like admiration for him.

"Come on! Come on!" he said, quivering with impatience.

"Knock it off! Keep your damn trap shut!" said Frank savagely.

He tried to start the motor. It spluttered damply.

"Hurry it up, for God's sake!" said Hal, who was now almost weeping. "They're coming! Talk about sitting ducks! We can't fight—there's too many of them!"

Four prison guards appeared. Three were holding revolvers and stopped to open fire. But they were too far away to hit anything.

The fourth had a tommy gun crooked under one arm. He at least had realized that to bring down the fugitives he had to be within range.

He shouted to his colleagues to stop wasting bullets and ran onto the jetty.

Frank swore and turned the engine over for the third time. It caught. He opened the throttle.

Suddenly the launch was speeding over the water.

Frank had his back turned to the port. Hal, on the other hand, was sitting in the bow and saw the guard with the tommy gun get into position.

"Get down!" he yelled to Frank.

Frank turned instinctively to look behind him. A furious salvo came from the quayside. Bullets thudded into the wooden stern of the boat. Frank gave a cry and raised one hand to his head. When he lowered it, Hal was horrified to see that his comrade had a terrible wound to the forehead, just above the bridge of his nose. Blood was pouring out of it. Frank's face was already completely red with it.

But he did not seem to be in any pain. He went on holding the wheel.

There was a second volley of bullets but they dropped harmlessly behind them, cutting a furrow in the water.

"Hell's teeth!" muttered Frank. "What's happened to me, Hal?… I can't see a damned thing!… I felt like something hit me and…"

Hal stared at the wound without saying a word. He wondered how Frank could still speak and move with a hole like that in the lower part of his forehead.

"It was a bullet. It grazed you as you turned round," he said.

"Are you crazy? A bullet!… I'd be dead if I had taken a bullet in the forehead!"

Hal leant forward to get a closer look at the wound.

"It got you on the slant. It's nicked a chunk out of the bone at the top of your nose. You were lucky."

Some obscure instinct warned him that they were in great danger. He turned and saw that the boat was heading directly towards the breakwater of the port. Another ten metres and they would smash into the reinforced-concrete sea wall.

Hal threw himself on the steering wheel and turned it hard. The boat almost flipped over. It fishtailed violently and the bow dipped so savagely that the propeller emerged from the water for a moment and, encountering no resistance, revolved with a tormented screech. The boat lurched agonizingly several times and shaved the breakwater so closely that it scraped its right side.

"What's happening?" asked Frank, who had almost been thrown overboard. "What's got into you?"

"What's got into me is that we damn near crashed into the breakwater."

"I can't see zilch," growled Frank.

"That's because your eyes are covered with blood. Come on, move over so I can take the wheel."

"Where are the screws now?" asked Frank.

"Standing on the far side of the port… they're all arriving in a hurry but they can kiss goodbye to the idea of catching us now."

Frank was using his sleeve to staunch the blood which was pouring down his face.

"Is there a motor launch in the harbour?" he asked. "If there is, we've had it."

Hal looked.

"Can't see one," he said. "Anyway, if there was you can bet your boots they'd be aboard it already!"

"True…"

The quayside was now black with people.

The crowd was watching them the way people watch a sensational spectacle.

"We got a full house," said Hal. "Dammit, the swine think they're at the circus!"

He glanced at Frank, who was leaning forward with his head on his sleeve, which had now turned completely red.

"How do you feel?" he asked.

"Pretty bad, thanks… It burns like there was a red-hot poker on it and I've got shooting pains in my head."

"Hang on, I'll wash it with seawater in a while… The salt will help to sterilize it."

The engine was running smoothly and the port was dropping away behind them. Hal looked all round him. The sea was grey and calm, turning bluish as it neared the horizon. It was warm and the sun's rays fell gently on the surface of the water.

Coming hard on the heels of the narrow confines of the cell, this vastness unnerved him.

"What do we do next?" he asked.

"Where are we?" groaned Frank. "Don't head out to sea, whatever you do. We'll never reach America in this tub!"

"So?" asked Hal.

"Are we being followed?"

"Not for the moment…"

"Good… Turn in a wide arc and head back towards the coast… A quarter of an hour from now there'll be police launches on our tail… And customs, the whole tribe… We get to the coast and we lie low. Shame I got hit…"

"It won't be problem," said Hal without conviction.

And so saying he took a look at Frank's forehead, which was lathered with purplish froth.

9

"You'll run out of juice," said Frank.

"Think so?"

"You'd better believe it!... Can't you hear it misfiring?... Change course now, because if we don't we'll find ourselves adrift on this cockleshell boat."

Hal peered at the coast, which was now close. It was almost dark and the sea was turning choppy. Not far away was a line of steep, high cliffs.

"The coast," he said. "We're almost there, but I'm wondering where we can land."

Suddenly he went quiet.

Anxiously, Frank asked:

"What's the matter?"

"I can see lights."

"Are they moving?"

"No... It's a house... The windows are lit."

"Fine. Try to land near there."

Hal obeyed. He saw a kind of small harbour where a sailing boat and a motor launch were lying at anchor.

It was a private harbour belonging to a very large property.

He described the lie of the land to his companion. Oddly enough, after Frank had got hit, he seemed to Hal to have become more experienced and capable than he had been before. It was now to this blind man that he instinctively looked to lead them wherever their crazy caper might take them.

"Take her in gently," said Frank. "We'll hole up in the grounds of this mansion... Perhaps we'll find some clothes and maybe something to eat."

"Do you believe in miracles?" said Hal sarcastically.

"There are times when you have to..."

Suddenly the engine cut out.

"Did you turn off the petrol supply?"

"No," said Hal, "she died a natural death. No more juice."

"Are we far from land?"

"We're there!"

"OK. Help me to get out."

With great difficulty they eventually got back on dry land.

"Now, give the boat a good shove!..." said Frank. "It don't matter where she goes... The tide's going out and it'll take her God only knows where and that suits us fine."

Without warning he gave a hiccup and collapsed onto the sand.

"What's up with you?" said Hal.

But Frank was gasping for breath and could not answer.

Hal took off the coat of his prison fatigues and used it as a canvas bucket to fetch seawater, which he splashed gently on his comrade's face. The salt made Frank's wound sting and he groaned:

"Stop, you're hurting me... Everything's gone all blurry; it's a God-awful feeling... Maybe I'm going to snuff it, what do you think, Hal?"

Hal wrapped his wet coat over Frank's forehead.

"Don't be a dope. The damage to your nose is something or nothing. Give it three days and it will have all healed up."

"Where will we be in three days?"

"Stop making a fuss. Where would the charm of life be if you kept worrying about the future?"

He stood up and looked around him. They were on the edge of a spinney of stunted trees. Through the spinney wound a sandy path that led to the house.

It was an imposing building, in the English style.

Hal hesitated.

He had to do something. With a wounded man in tow and every police force in France snapping at their heels the situation looked dire.

He made up his mind: "Listen, I'm going to leave you in a safe spot and go and see what I can find…"

"What exactly?" asked Frank.

"Anything. We've got nothing, so whatever I can get hold of we may be able to use."

"I know what you're going to do," said Frank.

"Then you know more than I do."

"You're going to leave me here, you bastard! Because I'm no use to you! You're going to beat it all by yourself—this is your big chance…"

Hal took his hand. His thumb felt his comrade's pulse: it was racing.

"Get a grip," he said. "Look, if I wanted to run out on you, I'd tell you. Wait for me and don't make a noise…"

He grabbed him round the waist and chivvied rather than helped him to move under the low branches of a tree.

"I'll be back, OK?"

He walked off in the direction of the house. The nearer he got the more clearly he could make out snatches of music, loud voices and laughter… There was clearly a reception being held that evening in the house by the sea.

"This," thought Hal, "must be my lucky day. When people are having fun, they don't pay as much attention to what's going on around them!"

He prowled around the building. Open windows allowed him to see into a huge drawing room full of people, all in evening dress.

He went all round the house, locating the usual offices and outbuildings. He found the servants' hall. The door was open and there was no one inside. A table groaned with trays, each laden with a heap of good things: canapés, sandwiches and an assortment of other appetizers. Bottles of champagne and whisky were cooling in tubs filled with ice.

He hesitated, then flattened himself against the wall, just outside the door. His whole body was tense. Just as he was about to step inside, a door opened and a servant in a white jacket walked in, carrying dirty glasses. He deposited them in a sink for washing up, picked up a full tray and went out again.

Hal rushed in almost immediately on the heels of the man. He seized a bottle of whisky, grabbed two sandwiches and ran back out into the night. He was pleased with himself and happy with his haul. Without waiting, he bit into one of the sandwiches.

Treading quietly, he started walking back to the spot in the grounds where he had left Frank. He got a fright when he saw a white-clad figure standing in front of his comrade.

Frank was half-kneeling and holding out one hand to the woman while he stammered in a helpless voice:

"Is that you, Hal?"

Hal saw that the figure was a young woman in evening dress. It seemed most likely that she had come out for a breath of fresh air.

Frank's low groans must have attracted her attention as she strolled. Insofar as the light of the moon allowed Hal to make out, she was blonde and young, with a good figure and pretty face.

Frank persisted, though he did not dare raise his voice:

"Hello? Is that you, Hal? Is there anyone there?"

Hal gently placed the barrel of his revolver against the low-cut back of the young woman's dress.

"Yes, Frank, there's someone here," he said softly.

She gave a cry and turned round.

Her eyes went from Hal's hard-set face down to the gun he was pointing at her at arm's length.

"Keep your mouth shut," he murmured. "There are three bullets left in this gun and they could do some damage."

The woman kept her mouth shut. She seemed more surprised than afraid.

"Who is it?" asked Frank.

"A nurse," said Hal.

The young woman was breathing with difficulty.

"Are you the two men who escaped? The ones the radio was talking about earlier?" she asked.

"I think you could say that," said Hal. "Unless there's been an outbreak of escaping today."

"What is—"

He cut her short with a gesture made all the more persuasive by the gun he was still holding.

"Be quiet! I ask the questions. When you've got one of these in your hand, you're entitled to do the talking... Who are you?"

"I own this place..."

He looked at her then gave an unpleasant laugh.

"My little chum here has been in the wars. A bullet wound low on his forehead. I think it should be disinfected right away and that he should be given a shot of quinine. Now, I'm betting there's a well-stocked medicine cabinet in your bathroom?"

"There is."

"Let's go and see!"

"Hal! You're crazy!" Frank said with a groan. "We'll get killed if we set foot in there!"

"Don't worry about it—the lady knows her way around the place. If she wants to save her skin—and her skin is much too pretty for her not to care about it—everything will be just fine.

"Will you do it?" he asked her.

"Follow me," she said.

Hal hooked one of Frank's arms over his shoulder to support his faltering steps.

"Wait!" he said. "I found a bottle of whisky—it's good stuff! Get some of it down you; it'll put lead in your pencil."

Frank sucked greedily from the bottle.

"You quaffed that like it was lemonade," said Hal admiringly.

"It does a power of good," muttered Frank.

They followed the woman as far as the servants' hall. When they reached the door through which Hal had entered, they waited while the same waiter came in and left.

"Let's go!" said Hal.

All three passed through the room and reached some back stairs, which took them up to the floor above. The woman led the way.

She was not afraid. Hal, who could now see her in the light, could not help liking what he saw. He thought she had class.

They entered a luxurious bedroom. Hal closed the door behind them and turned the key in the lock.

"Ah!" he said. "If you only knew how good it feels to be in civilized surroundings again. Sit on the bed, Frank, it's just in front of you!"

Frank sat down. The woman went into the bathroom and they heard her opening the sliding door of a medicine cabinet.

She returned with several small glass bottles and some gauze.

"Give!" said Hal. "I'll fix him up."

"I'll do it better than you can," the young blonde woman said firmly.

"Oh? Well, go ahead then."

She began by disinfecting the wound, then blew a puff of a sulfamide-based powder over it. Finally, she bandaged it very tightly.

"I'll be damned!" muttered Hal. "You're good at this! It's your Red Cross lady side showing, am I right?"

She just gave a shrug, which raised Hal's sensitive hackles.

"Oh, suit yourself!"

She returned to her medicine cabinet, dropped two pills in a glass of water and came back.

"Drink this!" she told Frank, putting the glass in his hand.

Frank hesitated.

"Is it all right, Hal?" he asked helplessly.

"Don't be a clown!" joked Hal. "Listen, this lady here isn't the sort of hostess that slips a wounded soldier a dose of rat poison!"

He stood up, crossed to a wardrobe and opened it. He gave a cry of delight.

"Talk about a land of plenty!" he said. "There's everything here you need to dress up as Prince Charming. You'd never think there were men who owned so many clothes."

He took out a blue serge suit.

"About my size. The trousers aren't quite the ticket, but I only have to let them down as far as they'll go. And shirts, Frank! Silk too! Makes you feel like you're the Duke of Windsor when you see a wardrobe like this!"

He chose a suit for his friend and helped him into it.

"Listen, lady, if you're shy just turn round," he said.

But the woman did not budge. She watched as the men undressed with muted, if slightly suspect curiosity.

"Like that, is it?" smiled Hal. "If it gives you a kick we've got no objection to you getting your money's worth!"

Once Frank had changed, Hal undressed and pulled on a pair of trousers and a turtleneck sweater. But it was a bit tight. To get his arm into the sleeve he had to put the revolver down. It was then that he understood why the blonde had not turned round and looked the other way. Quick as a flash, she lunged and snatched the gun. Then with a steady hand she pointed it at Hal.

"Aha!" he said, as his face dropped. "Seems like things are getting complicated."

"What's going on?" asked Frank, who sensed that something was wrong.

"The lady's just grabbed the shooter."

"You dumb bastard!" said Frank.

"Language!" said Hal. "That sort of talk isn't fit for a lady's ears!"

"Don't move!" said the woman.

She seemed to be thinking and watched them in an odd way, as if she were in two minds.

At that moment, there was a knock at the door.

The two men froze. The blonde smiled. She crossed to the door and reached for the knob, but then had second thoughts and asked:

"Who is it?"

A polite voice murmured:

"It's Julien, Madame. The master has sent me up to ask if you would care to come downstairs. Madame's guests are getting anxious…"

She hesitated again: it was probably the painful sight of Frank's face which decided the fate of both men.

Without taking his eyes off her, Hal picked up the second sandwich, which he had put on the marble mantelpiece, and took a bite.

"Tell my husband that I'll be down very shortly," she said.

The servant mumbled a hasty "Very good, Madame" and went away.

The woman tossed the gun onto the counterpane.

"Get out. And be quick about it."

"Is this your week for doing good works?" asked Frank.

"No. My birthday… Make the most of it… Go before I have second thoughts… Women are always changing their minds: everyone knows that."

Hal hurriedly snatched back the revolver and slipped it into his belt.

"Come on, Frank," he said, "and say thank you to the kind lady… It's thanks to the Good Lord himself that she crossed our Goddam path!"

Taking the wounded man's arm again, he stepped out into the corridor, but not before giving the young woman an eloquent look.

10

When they got outside and felt the night wind, Frank heaved a sigh.

"That was a near one!"

"Dead right!"

"What got into her, do you think, for her to give us a present like that?"

"She told you herself. It's her birthday."

"When it's your birthday, you get presents, you don't give them."

"Oh women have a different way of looking at life. Perhaps she felt sorry for us…"

"You mean sorry for me?" said Frank.

"In what way sorry?"

"Do you think I've gone blind?"

Hal shrugged his shoulders.

"Of course not!"

"You don't sound very convinced."

"Listen," said Hal, "now's not the time to start worrying about your problems."

"What are we going to do, Hal?"

"Well… we get out of here, agreed?"

"Agreed. But how?"

Hal looked carefully all round him.

"There's a whole lot of cars parked over there. Maybe we could steal one?"

"Oh sure, and run straight into the arms of the cops? Trust me, there'll be roadblocks everywhere."

"All right then, brains, have you got any better ideas?"

"Wait a minute…" said Frank. "Yes! We go back to the sea. The tide was in when we landed, right?"

"Yes."

"So it will have started going out by now?"

"Probably."

"Good. If it's going out, we can start walking along the base of the cliffs. It's perfect. The cops will never think of looking for us along the shore… In their tiny minds there are sheer cliffs and the sea below… It won't occur to them that you can walk along the foot of the cliffs for eight hours!"

Hal gave his comrade an admiring look.

"You're full of ideas, and that's a fact!"

"I got ideas, sure have," said Frank.

And as he took the arm of his fellow fugitive, he repeated: "If it's ideas you want, I'm your man!"

They were almost dead on their feet when a faint dawn began to break far out at sea. Walking on fallen rocks and shingle is exhausting. Several hours of staggering along, of sleepwalking progress across mounds of scree, had sapped the last of their strength.

Frank dropped down onto the accumulation of round black stones which turned the shore into a virtual moonscape.

"I've had it!" he said. "I'm all in!"

Hal sat down beside him for a moment, then snorted:

"Pull yourself together, man! Sooner or later we'll find a place to hide. So far, we've been doing just fine… You came up with the great idea of walking along the shore. Brilliant!

And we're not leaving any tracks either. The only thing is that any minute now the tide will start to turn and we'll have to find somewhere safe…"

"Let it turn! Let the sea come all the way up and then you won't have to go looking for the perfect hiding place—you'll have it here, deep beneath the waves! There's no better bed than the seabed."

Hal's answer was to grab Frank under the arms and force him back onto his feet.

"Hey! You're a grown man! So start walking!"

"Listen, Hal, it's not just being exhausted… I can't see. You've got no idea what it's like walking in the pitch black… with all these damn rocks that move when you step on them!"

"I dare say," murmured Hal.

While they talked they'd set off again along the line of the shore.

The light was strengthening. A zone of deep purple marked the point on the horizon where the sun would soon come up. The air was crisp and cold… Gulls flew over them, gliding with easy grace and uttering their raucous cries which hurt the ears.

Hal looked despairingly over the long stretch of shingle, the sheer cliff fringed at the top with stunted grass, the foaming sea as it slowly encroached on their closed world. He was beginning to lose heart. What was the use of staggering on, of the bursts of energy required of them and the sudden fits of crazy hope?

They had set themselves an impossible task. They were doomed from the start. There was no way out.

Frank collapsed again.

"Jesus falls for the second time," he muttered, and then added: "I'm thirsty."

"Here, try a swig of whisky," suggested Hal, who had taken good care not to leave the bottle behind.

Frank raised it to his lips. The whisky tasted very strong. It coursed through his belly and a warm sensation spread right through him. It felt good, very good. It felt as good as death when we want it and it comes to us…

"Good God!" exclaimed Hal.

"What's up?" croaked Frank.

"I don't know if I'm seeing things, but I can make out an island a couple of hundred metres farther along."

"An island?"

"A small one… There's a sort of little hill on it and a few trees…"

"It's a mirage," sneered Frank.

"It's real!"

Hal scoured the horizon.

"Yes, a small island… At low tide you can probably walk there without getting your feet wet, or not very. At the moment I can see water, not much… all round it."

"And at high tide it's completely underwater!"

"Did you ever see an island with trees on it that was completely submerged?"

"No, you're right."

"So come on, man!"

Frank groaned as he got to his feet.

They turned and walked straight towards the sea, setting their backs resolutely to the cliffs.

At first, they continued picking their way awkwardly over rock and shingle, but soon they found themselves on sand and started walking smoothly and soundlessly.

"Is that better for you?" said Hal.

"Yes."

"You're enjoying walking on this, aren't you, old buddy? It's like strolling on velvet!"

"You're right, just like velvet," said Frank, echoing the thought, infected by his comrade's high spirits.

"An island," said Hal, "is the ideal place to hide. We couldn't have hoped to find anything better! We can lie low here and live like kings for a while…"

"Not exactly like kings… How are we really going to live?"

"There's shellfish. What do you reckon? Seafood's very nourishing, you know."

"What'll we drink?"

"If there are trees, there's bound to be fresh water."

"You think so?"

"I'm certain… we'll wait until you're better. By then, the manhunt will have gone off the boil. The good thing about news is that there's new news every day… When you're on your feet again, we'll move on…"

"Aren't you the optimist!"

They walked on in silence. The splash of the waves grew louder. Suddenly, Frank stopped.

"Hey!"

Hal knew what was bothering him.

"You're right," he said, "we're sinking."

They walked on a little farther, but with difficulty, because instead of sand they were now crossing a muddy, treacherous area which grasped and sucked at their legs like some giant mouth.

Frank had just sunk halfway up his thighs in shifting mud.

He started screaming like a madman and flapped his arms wildly. His screams were long, urgent and desperate… He exuded panic. It was contagious.

"Shut up, you dumb creep!… Don't you know that voices carry over water?"

"Help me, Hal! I'm sinking!"

"I'm sinking too! Lie flat and pull your legs out one after the other. I've worked it out. You've got to spread as much of your weight as you can over the surface!"

Frank groaned with the strain. He managed to free his right leg, which had not sunk in very far, but it was as if the left had been cemented in.

"Help me," he wept. "Help me! Don't leave me here!"

Then he passed out and lay face down in the ooze, which was covered by glutinous kelp.

"Here we go!" Hal muttered.

He crawled to where Frank lay and then, bracing himself as firmly as he could, pulled hard on the leg that was stuck fast. It came out slowly, making a sound like a bandage being removed.

Pulling so hard, Hal felt the last of his strength desert him. The effort was too great—he could do no more!

But then he was overtaken by a sudden frenzy.

Gasping, sweating, choking, cursing, he kept on pulling the still-imprisoned leg.

The brand-new suits they had taken from the personal wardrobe of the owner of the estate were now in a fine mess!

They had entirely lost their shape under a stucco of gelatinous mud.

"I've had enough of you!" said Hal through gritted teeth. "You make me sick! If I had any sense I'd just leave you here to die!"

Yet he went on pulling until he finally succeeded in freeing the submerged leg.

"Come on! Now do what I do!"

Frank did not move.

"Frank! Wake up, for Pete's sake! The tide's coming in! Come on, up you get! Pull yourself together, man!"

But Frank was still out cold. Hal put one ear to his comrade's chest. There was a regular heartbeat.

Reassured, he rolled Frank towards him until he was lying alongside his body. Then, spreading himself out on the sucking sand, and with a heave of which he would not have believed himself capable, he managed to haul the body up and onto his own back. But pressed down by such a heavy load, he found it impossible to move forward. He was being crushed by Frank's dead weight.

"Damn him!…" he gasped. "Goddam bastard!"

He moved his arms and legs ridiculously, like a frog, in an attempt to crawl over the mire. He succeeded only in getting his feet tangled in lengths of seaweed, which wound themselves round his ankles like snakes.

"I got it all wrong," he thought. "I said we'd be able to get to the island at low tide. But in fact you can only reach it at high tide and by boat."

But putting the case like that gave him an idea. If he couldn't move, why not wait for the sea to do it for him? It was coming in slowly and surely. All he'd have to do then would be to swim to the accommodating shore of the island, which he could see just there, just a few strokes away.

He waited on the sand while the day grew lighter all round him. His only worry now was that they might be seen from the clifftop. But so early in the morning, that was not very likely.

And so the time passed. Hal began to get drowsy. He felt oppressed by Frank's breathing but even so he fell asleep in that position. He was woken by a tongue of water. It licked him gently in the face.

He waited, half propped up on his elbows. The water continued to rise. Soon, it overtook him. He sat up. Then the water was up to his chest. Now he could paddle.

He stretched out on the water. He tried moving his arms and legs. Then he was floating. In a moment of jubilation, he laughed. It was a solitary, grim laugh. He gripped Frank under his lifeless arms and pulled him against his chest. Then on his back, he kicked out for the shore.

It took him less time than he had estimated to cross the stretch of sea. Eventually he landed on a beach of firm sand and staggered out of the water, dragging his comrade with him.

He felt that he too was about to pass out.

"Die, you bastard!" he muttered as he let go of Frank's clenched hands.

Then he lay flat on his back and looked unblinkingly up at the new day's too-red sun.

PART III

Beauty 2

11

They regained consciousness almost simultaneously. It was probably the sun beating down on their faces that roused them from the comatose state into which they had sunk.

They both opened their eyes. Convoys of wispy clouds drifted slowly on a high breeze which could not be felt at sea level.

Frank stammered:

"Where are we?"

"On the island," murmured Hal.

"How come?"

"I dragged you here."

"Thanks," said Frank. "You're a real brother!"

"A brother wouldn't have done that for you!"

"OK, so you're a good pal who looks out for me on account of me being delicate!"

Hal spat out the sand which had accumulated in his mouth.

"I wish you were dead," he mused. "I've had a bellyful of you and your stupid comments."

"In that case you should have left me there in the mud... I was caught like a rat in a trap! The sea would have drowned me..."

"It's not fair," grumbled Hal. "I risk my life to save yours. You're about as strong as a newborn slug but the first words you come out with are a put-down..."

There was a silence.

"Those are rain clouds," said Hal, who had been watching the masses of grey as they scudded across the sky.

"Yes, and they're going to drop their load on people, and why not?… I wish they would and wipe them all out, the whole lot of them."

"Me too…"

Hal got to his knees and looked around him.

"You sure this is an island?" asked Frank.

"You bet. If you feel like doing a Robinson Crusoe, now's your chance… Well I'll be… Good God!"

"What?"

Hal stared at his companion. The bandage had been torn off Frank's head and his eyes were now fully open.

"Say, can you see properly?"

With one movement, Frank sprang to his feet.

"I can!" he exulted. "I can see! I can see! And there was me thinking I'd gone blind! Isn't that tremendous?"

"You bet!… Come on, this way!"

They walked across the short grass which started where the beach ended.

There was a low rise in the land on which stood a number of stunted trees. Clear water ran down one side of the hillock. Hal flung himself face down… It was drinkable.

"Drink!" he cried.

Frank followed his example.

"This is amazing!" he said, weeping with relief. "Wonderful!"

He was greatly affected by everything. The recovery of his eyesight especially, but also this sweet, fresh water, the awesome quiet and their isolation.

He held out both arms to Hal.

"You're a real friend, you know," he murmured.

"Don't give me that stuff!" said Hal. "Don't get all

sentimental on me… I'm not having it!… Get a grip! God, you're so slow!"

And he strode off, greatly restored by the rest he'd just had and the water he'd drunk. Frank trotted behind him, breathing hard.

"Mustn't be too rough on me… Listen…"

Hal stopped suddenly, but not because he was waiting for Frank. Not far from the copse stood a small fisherman's hut built of mud bricks. It was in a very poor state and it was obviously a long time since the roof, with its tiles made of flattened tin cans, had been repaired.

He made a beeline for it, followed by Frank, who whimpered happily, like a puppy dog.

Hal pushed open the door made of reused timber. It creaked mournfully and spiders fled. Inside were a makeshift table, two benches, a heap of dried seaweed and shelves, on which were stacked a quantity of tins.

"Here, rest up," he said, pointing to the seaweed. "It's not the Plaza but it sure is better than a prison cell…"

Frank flopped onto the dried kelp. Hal hurriedly ran his eye over the tins. Most were empty, but to his delight he found matches in one, dried haricot beans in another and a small quantity of coffee in a third. Moreover, there was a bag of rye flour leaning against one of the large stones which made up a rudimentary fireplace.

"We've struck it rich!" he said. "Wait and see what sort of chow I am about to rustle up for you!"

He took the largest of the empty tins and went off to get water.

"Some tasty gravy and dumplings made with this flour will be a meal fit for a king."

When he came back he was carrying an armful of dead wood.

"What do you reckon this place is?" said Frank.

"I'll tell you… There must have been fishermen on this island once. Then they abandoned it. From time to time campers would come here and play desert islands during their holidays. They're the ones who left the grub."

"We couldn't have found a better place," sighed Frank.

"Too damn right," agreed Hal. "We couldn't have."

12

They spent a troubled night. Frank's temperature shot up
several times. He grew delirious and Hal got up often to give
him a cooling drink of water. He regretted he hadn't taken
a supply of medicines from the villa. The blonde woman
would have let him have them as willingly as she had given
the suits.

In addition to Frank's groaning there was the loud beating of the sea all around them. It was as if they were on a
motionless boat in the middle of a storm. The bright beam
of a distant lighthouse flickered on and off all around with
sickening regularity.

Hal did not get to sleep until early morning, when again
it was his comrade who woke him.

"Hal!" he cried. "Hal!"

With the instant reflexes of a man who is hunted, Hal sat
up clear-headed the moment he was awake.

"What?"

"It's back; it's started again; I can't see… This time I'm
really blind!"

"Don't talk rubbish!"

"It's not rubbish! I tell you I can't see properly!"

Hal examined the wound. It did not look good and was
beginning to fester. Overcoming his distaste he eased it open.
The bullet had struck more deeply than he had thought. It
had probably clipped the optic nerve.

"I'm going to clean you up," he said. "There's a bit of pus
in it. You're going to have to keep a bandage over your eyes,

Frank—you've probably damaged an optic nerve or something... You'll find it more restful being in the dark."

Frank said nothing.

He bore uncomplainingly the basic ministrations of his companion in adversity. Hal poured whisky on the wound and bound it with a piece of the lining of his jacket.

"There you go," he said. "Don't fiddle with it. You've probably got a bit of a temperature, but that'll pass..."

"A bit of a temperature!" said Frank. "Come off it, you could fry an egg on my forehead!"

He lay down on his seaweed bed. The hut smelt of iodine. Hal looked all round and felt uneasy. The bottom line was that they were in a fix!... It wasn't his idea of freedom!

He went outside.

"Hey!" bawled Frank.

"What do you want?"

"Where are you going?"

"I'm going to get us something to eat."

"Where?"

"Never heard of the infinite riches of the sea?"

"I'm not hungry!"

"You're so self-centred!..." Hal snapped. "Just because you're in a bad way you think the world has stopped turning! Well I'm good and hungry, you know... A griping hunger, like there's a rat gnawing at my guts! And all the water I can drink won't drown it, cos rats can swim..."

He picked up an old canvas bucket he found in one corner of the hut.

"Go on, get some sleep—it'll set you up... When the body's sick, you've got to let it get on with it. It'll cure itself..."

Hal left the hut and walked towards the sea.

The previous evening, their isolation had seemed a blessing but now it oppressed him. He had an unsettling sense that a danger graver than that represented by the police was hanging over him.

He reached the rocks intending to look for crabs. It was the first time he'd ever tried an activity of this kind. All he knew about hunting for crabs was what he had read in books, and that didn't amount to much.

But hunger sharpens the wits and Hal was very hungry indeed.

He ventured right to the water's edge. He could just make out the mainland through a greyish fog, in which seabirds flew, shrieking their raucous, plaintive cries.

He began lifting stones. But crabs are wily creatures. They stay beneath the stone as it is being moved or else promptly bury themselves in the sand.

It was not long before Hal's fingers were covered with blood. At first, he could not understand why. He examined his hands, which looked as if they had been sliced by small razor blades, and saw that every large stone he moved was ringed with a collar of tiny broken shells with wickedly sharp edges. In the water he could not feel the tiny cuts.

That was the sea, in a word: a mine of wonderment and deceit. This discovery led him to proceed with more care and he found crabs.

They teemed at that spot. Soon he had half a bucketful. The canvas receptacle was soon full of squirming life.

Cheered by his haul, he returned to the hut. Frank was dozing.

Hal put water to heat on the fire in the rudimentary hearth and waited until it boiled before putting the crabs into it.

"Catch anything?" asked Frank.

"Sure did. We're going to have us a good feed, that I promise you."

"But I told you, I'm not hungry."

"So you did but you'll have to force yourself unless you want to starve to death... They say it's a good way to die. Life just seems to fade away, like water draining from a bucket with a hole in it."

He made Frank eat the meat of a few crabs which he prepared for him. It was good eating.

"You got to eat it straight away, where it's caught," grinned Hal. "Crabs crawl but they don't travel!"

The day passed without Hal noticing. He set about organizing their life on the island as if it were going to last a long time.

There were unsuspected riches in the hut if a man had an inventive turn of mind.

For example, outside, on a pile of old rubbish, he found a small drum of old engine oil left over from the time when a motorboat had been serviced there.

He was delighted with his find, for it solved the problem of lighting, at least for a time.

With an empty sardine tin and a length of twisted cotton he was able to fashion an oil lamp.

On the beach he found limpets clinging to the rocks under the seaweed. He prised them loose with an old knife blade. When he had collected enough, he returned to cook them.

"Are we going to be eating shellfish and crabs all the time we're here?" asked Frank.

"Sure thing!... We'll save the *poulet chasseur* for later... Seafood's not bad. It's got phosphorus in it."

They ate a rather meagre dinner, which left their stomachs unsatisfied. Frank's wound remained unchanged. Hal cleaned it up again with whisky.

"It's a shame to waste good booze like that," he said. "Still, it disinfects this nasty injury of yours."

Frank was depressed because he still could not see. He felt he was sinking into a black pit... It was distressing and it also hurt like blazes.

"Buck your ideas up," said Hal. "Lie down and try to get some shut-eye."

"But I've spent all day on my back. I don't feel sleepy."

"You've still got a temperature. You need rest... And since you are at least able to get your head down, you might as well make the most of it. When you're back on your feet again, we'll leave this place one fine evening, as the tide comes in."

"And where'll we go?"

"Wherever you want."

They remained a moment without speaking. The crude wick gave out a ghostly light. It smoked and filled the hut with a strong smell of engine oil.

"What was that?" Frank said, suddenly startled.

Hal frowned and listened, affected by a general sense of unease.

He noticed nothing unusual. He heard only the crash of the waves and the harsh cries of the birds.

"What's up?"

"I thought I heard…"

"What?"

"I don't know… shouts…"

"It's only the sea and the birds," said Hal in a neutral voice. "You're on edge tonight, that's what it is… You've got to pull yourself together!"

"Pulling yourself together's not easy in the dark," grumbled Frank. "In the pitch black I have this feeling that I'm surrounded by all sorts of dangers."

Hal's voice sounded hollow when he objected:

"Mustn't start imagining things, Frank. I'm here… and I've got the gun… There's still three bullets in the spout."

"They've been in the sea," Frank pointed out.

"No problem… There was a tobacco pouch in this suit, it's made of nylon… I wrapped the piece in it."

"Good thinking… What did you do with the tobacco that was in the pouch?"

"I slung it. Why? Would you have wanted it?"

"No, I don't smoke."

"Nor me," said Hal."

Frank got onto his knees on his seaweed bed.

"I'm scared," he said in a raw voice.

"Why? I told you: I've got a gun!"

"But that's it! That's why I'm scared."

"What do you mean?"

"If you wanted, if you took it into your head, Hal, you could get it out and point it at me and I wouldn't know… You could aim… You could take your time!"

Frank's teeth were chattering! Large beads of sweat ran down under the dressing. He was shaking.

Hal watched him panicking in amazement.

"Like now!" cried Frank. "This very minute! This very instant! I can feel you're taking aim at me! Yes!" he screamed. "I can feel it. The small muzzle of the revolver, I can sense it... Don't shoot! Please! I'm begging you!"

"You're crazy," said Hal sadly.

"Gimme your hands!..." Frank demanded. "Both of them... Now!"

Hal reached gently for his hands. Frank felt them frantically all over, then calmed down. At length, he gave a long sigh and murmured.

"Jeez... I was really scared!... How stupid is that?"

"Too damn right it's stupid!" muttered Hal. "Afraid of me!... After all I've done for you!"

"I'm sorry... You have no idea what it's like!..."

"But I do, Frank, I really understand..."

"You can't," said Frank. "You've got to be blind to understand... Blind! Do you think it'll last?"

"Of course it won't... It's your wound that's festering. When we get back on dry land you'll get yourself off to see an optician."

"That's not going to happen for a while."

"No, but it'll happen soon! On the whole it's all gone pretty well up to now, except for you getting winged, so let's just wait till the heat has died down..."

Frank seemed calmer. But judging by the way his hands shook, Hal guessed he was shivering with fever.

"If only I'd grabbed some of those damn pills!" he said to himself. "The last thing we want now is for septicaemia to invite itself to the picnic."

He wondered what he'd do if Frank's condition worsened... Should he let him die in the hut or, instead, leave him, find a phone and raise the alarm? But they'd only make Frank better so that they could send him to the guillotine... So...

"Is it dark outside?" asked Frank.

"Has been for at least an hour..."

"Have you lit the lamp?"

"Sure."

"I don't want it lit!" cried Frank. "I can't stand it!"

"Why?"

"I don't want you to have the light on, Hal. It's bad enough during the day. I can't prevent you from seeing during the day, but at night... You've got to leave the night to me!"

"You're a real tyrant!" said Hal.

"So put it out! Put it out, do you hear? Knowing there's a light shining that I can't see is making me ill!"

"For Pete's sake!" cried Hal. "What do you expect me to do in the dark? I'm not blind!"

"We can talk," sobbed Frank.

Hal knew that he was dealing with the ramblings of a sick man.

"OK, OK," he sighed.

He blew hard as people do when extinguishing a flame but in reality it was to fool his sick partner.

"Is it out?" asked Frank.

"Sure is."

Frank thought hard for something to say, failed and sat down on his makeshift mattress. Hal found a yellowed sheet of old newspaper on the floor and began reading it to pass the time. He was not ready for sleep and was gripped by a vague gloom which he felt like a pain inside him.

"What are you doing?" Frank, who had been listening, asked suddenly.

"Oh... nothing much."

Frank leapt to his feet. He groped his way to the table.

"You're making paper rustle," he said.

He felt Hal's face, his hands, then the old sheet of newspaper.

"You bastard!" he cried. "You didn't put the lamp out! You're reading!"

Losing patience, Hal thumped the table with his fist.

"That's enough!" he shouted.

Frank stopped yelling. He just stood, not moving, attentive and contrite.

"You'd better be careful!" Hal went on, his anger making him stumble over his words. "Listen to me, and listen good! I'm starting to get riled!"

Frank pleaded:

"No! Don't!"

He tried to justify himself.

"You got to understand, Hal," he whined, "I can't see anything!"

Pathetically he asked:

"What are you reading?"

"The serial in an old newspaper that was lying around the place..."

"Is it any good?"

"Sensational!... Top notch!"

"Tell me the story!" said Frank, bursting with impatience as if he were expecting some crucial revelation. "Tell me now!"

"It's about the daughter of this big oil tycoon who gets knocked up thanks to a criminal, as if it's only criminals that put it about…"

"And?"

"She gets her maid to say the kid is hers. Problem sorted! Jeez, that must have taken a lot of dreaming up!"

"What happens after that?"

"How should I know?… It's a serial and you've got to wait for the next episode, like all serials. You'll just have to work it out for yourself. You don't need to be rich to have imagination!"

Frank gave a thin, fearful smile indistinguishable from a sob.

"Hal," he said suddenly, "give me the gun."

"Are you off your head? You want to kill yourself?"

"No."

"Then what? It's all a blind man can do with a shooter: turn it against himself…"

"I want it!" persisted Hal. "I'm scared."

"Sure," said Hal. "And I'd be even more scared if I saw you waving it around!"

"At least give me the bullets…"

"If I did that, it wouldn't be a gun any more… Suppose we got in a jam…"

"Give me the bullets!" snivelled Frank.

Hal sighed. His partner was being a real drag. He opened the chamber and took out the clip. With his thumb he removed two bullets.

"Here," he said, holding them out to Frank. "If that's what you want…"

Frank grabbed the two bullets the way a drug addict grabs a fix of snow.

He felt them with his fingers, and his jaw muscles tightened.

"You dirty son of a bitch! You've only given me two and a moment ago you said yourself there were three left!"

He held out his hand. His fingers curled and uncurled greedily, clumsily. Hal stared at them and thought of the crabs he'd caught that morning.

Angrily, he ejected the last bullet from the clip into his hand, felt the weight of it there and reluctantly thrust it hard into Frank's palm.

"Ah, you're hurting me!" said Frank, wincing.

"Yeah, and you're hurting me too, Frank… Feel happy now, I hope?"

"Not happy—safe."

"You damned!…"

Frank held out one hand to shut him up… He twisted his head slightly and his slack mouth showed how hard he was concentrating.

"Sh!" he said.

"You're completely off your rocker!" cried Hal, throwing himself face down on the bed of seaweed.

"Shut up!…" said Frank urgently. "Can't you hear it?"

"Sure, I can hear a clown talking and it's seriously pissing me off…"

"There was someone walking about outside," said Frank.

He had spoken with such conviction that Hal was not able to protest with the appropriate vigour.

"Oh," he said after a moment, "you and your imagination!…"

"I'm not imagining anything," whispered Frank. "When you can't see your ears get sharper. This time, I'm quite sure of what I'm saying… Listen… There's somebody walking around out there…"

Hal felt icy fingers around his throat. He suddenly felt cold and alone.

He listened hard… and heard the mingled rumble of wind and sea.

But there were other sounds too… There were particular sounds made by the wind. And sounds produced by the ramshackle hut.

"You're raving," said Hal uncertainly.

Hal listened again.

Yes, he could hear it. It really did sound like footsteps. But it could not possibly have been footsteps. Silently, he repeated with savage intensity: "*It can't be! It cannot be!*" But what had made the stones move?

He had never felt so afraid in his life. He even realized that until this moment he had never felt true fear. Never!

"Give!" he said and held out his hand to Frank.

It was less an assertion than an order.

"Give what?" said blind Frank.

"The bullets! And quick about it…"

Frank shook his head.

"Three bullets? Come off it. What use would they be?"

"They could make three dead bodies when pointed in the right direction," said Hal. "So hand them back to me…"

Instead of obeying, Frank slipped the bullets into his trouser pocket.

"What's the use?" he said. "If it's the cops, we've had it."

"If it were the cops, they'd already have opened up with their sub-machine guns. This shack is just planks of wood... Do I need to draw a picture?..."

The two men stopped talking and listened. Their whole beings became a kind of radar: they picked up many sounds, they selected some and identified them in turn...

"Brace yourself," said Frank.

The footsteps had stopped outside the door.

13

"Maybe it isn't a man," Hal thought. "It could be an animal."

But what sort of animal would be wandering around an island not much bigger than the place de la Concorde?

"Go on, then! Open the door!" yelped Frank, who was now at his wits' end.

Hal stood up, hesitated, picked up the empty revolver by the barrel and walked to the door. All that could be heard now was the sound of the sea and the wind. He reached for the small metal bar which served as a latch, lifted it and pulled. The wind swept yowling into the hut.

Hal stood where he was, petrified by surprise. He was not afraid now but what he felt was just as strong. Standing in the doorway was a woman. And it was the woman from two nights before.

For one brief moment, it was as if the universe had neither frontiers nor reality. He stared at the blonde young woman. But she no longer had the strength to return his look. She staggered. Only then did he notice that her clothes—shorts and a woman's striped *marinière*—were torn and dripping with sea water.

The woman rested her forehead on the frame of the door. Her streaming wet hair hung down over her face.

"I must be dreaming..." thought Hal. "This can't be happening..."

Frank's anguished voice snapped him out of the state of uncertainty which had suddenly made his mind go blank.

"What's happening, Hal?... Tell me!... Hal, are you there?"

Getting no reply, Frank was starting to panic again.

"Answer, for God's sake! Hal! What's going on?"

"We've got a visitor," said Hal.

"A visitor!" cried Frank. "What are you talking about? Tell me!" The sound of his own voice was reassuring.

The blonde woman attempted to enter. She swayed and collapsed into Hal's arms.

He helped her into the hut and then kicked the door shut behind them. He took hold of her by the waist and laid her down on the table. Gently he teased the hair off her face, which was unnaturally pale. It was indeed the same woman who had come to their rescue the night before last.

"Yes," repeated Hal gravely, "a visitor… who comes by night, when the last hand is dealt… but whether she's the queen of hearts… or spades, we'll have to wait and see…"

"A woman?" said Frank, sitting up.

"Better: a pretty woman."

"Impossible!"

Frank sprang towards the table and almost went sprawling because the bench was in his way. Feverishly, he ran his hands over the unconscious woman.

"But it's true!" he said. "True! What's she playing at here, Hal?"

"She's playing dead," said Hal, uncorking the whisky bottle.

"Is she really dead?"

"No way! Women are tougher than that! She must have been out sailing hereabouts and her boat capsized. But guess who she is?"

Frank did not understand the question.

"How should I know?" he said.

"It's not so long ago that you were talking to her."

"Huh?"

Frank gave a start.

"It's that chick from the other day!"

"Ten out of ten!" said Hal as he pushed the neck of the bottle through the blonde woman's teeth.

"What are you doing to her?"

"Rendering unto Caesar what belongs to Caesar…"

He stopped speaking, for the woman had just opened her eyes and was murmuring something.

"What did she say?" asked Frank, jostling his partner.

"That it's awful."

"What's awful?"

"If you'd let her speak perhaps we'll find out."

Hal went on: "Here, give me a hand; we'll lay her on the ground—she'll be more comfortable, and so will we… It's unnerving to see a woman laid out on a table."

Frank felt around then gripped their visitor by the legs.

"Mind the bench!" said Hal. "That's it, one more step to the left!… Perfect… Now put her down."

He knelt down beside their recently arrived guest.

"Of all the!…" said Frank.

"Yeah. This is some coincidence!"

"Coincidence—you said it," echoed Frank.

He gave a laugh.

The woman looked up at them and in her still-uncertain eyes there was a degree of disbelief which equalled that of the two men.

"Evening," said Hal. "Well, well… Who'd have thought you'd miss us so much? You must have second sight…"

He stopped, for she was crying.

"Spare us the waterworks!"

"Leave her!" said Frank.

Hal smiled. The woman shrank back against the wall of the hut.

"You!" she said.

"Cut it out!" growled Frank. "Stop the play-acting and just tell us how you got here."

"I was out sailing with my husband… We went a long way out to sea, this afternoon. As we were coming back there was a sudden strong gust of wind and the boat was blown flat on its side. I was thrown into the sea…"

She stopped and put one hand over her eyes.

"Then what happened?" persisted Frank.

"I went under, my husband dived in, helped me back to the boat and told me to hang on to the hull. He tried to right the boat but couldn't manage it and then suddenly he just went straight down before my very eyes!…"

"RIP," murmured Hal.

"Shut your trap!" snapped Frank. "What happened then?"

"I clung on to the boat for as long as I could. I hoped the tide would carry the wreckage back to the coast but the opposite happened. The wind started blowing me out to sea. I knew I'd die unless I did something! Then, as it grew dark, I made out this island… Far, far away… I'm not a strong swimmer, but I decided to risk it."

"Risk is the word," said Frank.

"Many times I thought I'd go under. So I'd float on my back to steady myself and regain my strength. And in the end, I got here."

"Was that you shouting?"

"Yes."

"Aha!" said Frank to his partner. "See? I was right!"

"So you were," acknowledged Hal, before asking:

"There were just the two of you on board that damned boat of yours?"

"Yes."

"What about the guests you had back there?"

"They all left yesterday morning."

Hal stared at her coolly.

"Are you sure the unfortunate gust of wind wasn't you?" he asked with a knowing smile.

She looked at him uncomprehendingly.

"What do you mean?"

"Your story don't ring true, darling—it sounds like it was cobbled together… The boat gets blown over, you start drowning, your hubby fishes you out and then he's the one who goes under… Next thing you get a trip across the Atlantic… And supposing you hadn't bothered about which way you were going, you'd have fetched up in New York harbour one of these fine days!"

She sat up.

"I forbid you to think such horrible things!"

"Oh! I'm just saying…"

"Herbert is dead!" she cried with genuine feeling. "We'd just had lunch and—"

"You said that it was getting on for evening when you started back, when the boat got turned over…"

"Because we'd been partying all night—"

"Ah! So you had! Many happy returns!"

The interruption did not appear to bother her. She seemed inert.

Meekly she went on:

"...We didn't have lunch and I'd had something made up for us which we'd eaten out at sea..."

She was crying quietly as she spoke.

"We must do something," she said.

"We can't do anything for someone who's been rolling around on the bottom of the sea for hours," said Frank. "There are plenty of fish down there. They can take care of him."

14

Hal looked at the woman carefully.

"Still," he said, "it could have been an accident after all. But to be honest, we don't give a damn if you did him in or not… It's just that it would be better if we were all on the same side, if you take my meaning. If only because it would make dealing with each other easier."

When she did not turn a hair at this, he went on, finding a guilty pleasure in provoking her.

"Because, of course, now that you're here, we can't afford the luxury of letting you go. Anyway, if you did try to leave the island, the odds that you would get sucked down in the mud or drowned would be shortissimo."

She was just beginning to understand her position, and there was a look of silent disapproval in her eye. She let out a groan.

"Is she good-looking?" asked Frank suddenly. He was breathing noisily.

The question took Hal by surprise. He looked at the woman again, now through different eyes.

"She could be my type…" he conceded. "You know, blonde, and eyes that could be violet at certain moments…"

"I wish I could see her," sighed Frank.

"You'll see her, all right! She'll be staying here for some time and you'll be cured long before the three of us go our separate ways."

The woman sat up.

"It's out of the question!" she said. "I won't! I don't want to!…"

Hal burst out laughing. He put one knee on the wooden bench and trimmed the smoking wick of his lamp.

"Listen, sweetie, in this life there are what are called circumstances. Circumstances decided that you should end up here with us... Well, you just have to put up with it. Fate... you see, there is such a thing... Fate, along with its sidekick, Chance! You helped us, so now it's our turn to help you. If we hadn't been here, you would now be by yourself on this island crying with cold and fear. Tomorrow you'd have tried to get back to the mainland on foot and you'd have gone to meet your maker with that pretty mouth of yours full of sand..."

"He's got the gift of the gab, hasn't he?" leered Frank.

"We wait!" said Hal.

She shook her head.

"Wait for what?"

"Wait until some time has gone by between us and the cops. The cops are just like everybody else. They've got memories, but believe me, memories are not intended just for remembering things, but, more importantly, for forgetting them!"

"Aw, put a sock in it!" cried Frank. "Have you finished rabbiting on? Lady, when he starts talking he gets drunk on his own words!" He went on: "Let's leave it at that! OK, so we make room for Widow Wossername here. I can't take any more of this!"

"Oh!" cried the woman.

She burst into tears... Her chest heaved, racked by sobbing... She fought for breath.

"You're being a bit hard on a young woman who was very nice to you," observed Hal.

Frank sidled up to him.

"You mustn't hold it against me," he said meekly.

He waved one hand about on the off chance of locating the woman. He touched her hair and started stroking it.

"Don't hold it against me…" he repeated. "I feel so down."

She freed herself with a horrified shrug. He felt the full force of the revulsion he inspired in her.

"You can cut that out!" Frank said angrily. "Don't get smart with me or I'll make sure you join your better half down among the fishes! I could do it, you bet I could, blind as I am!"

He lay down on his seaweed bed and starting crying with frustration.

Hal shrugged his shoulders and gathered up an armful of grass, which he spread out in another corner of the hut.

"Come, lie down here," he ordered the woman, "and cry your eyes out all you want if it makes you feel better. Tomorrow's another day and it won't be anything like today."

Head bowed, she did as she was told.

She was still asleep when the two men woke up next morning.

Frank tore off the bandage, which had stayed stuck over his wound. He blinked at the light.

"Can you see?" asked Hal, who was observing what he was doing.

"No," said Frank, "but there's hope… I can already tell the difference between light and dark… It's just like as if I were looking through frosted glass, if you follow me…"

Hall nodded: "Good. It's coming back slowly… And the wound isn't weeping any more—you're on the mend."

"Did you sleep well?" asked Frank.

"No."

"Me neither... Feeling that she was there, the scent of her... It's a long time since I had a woman anywhere within reach..."

"True," said Hal, "and it gets to you!"

"And how! My mouth goes dry just thinking about it!"

"She asleep?"

"Yeah," said Hal after glancing at the woman.

"Is she really good-looking?"

"A stunner!"

Frank sighed. He stood up and forced himself to open his half-closed eyes... But the pain started to come back.

"I'll have to bathe my eyes in water that's been boiled," he said. "That'll do them good, won't it?"

"A power of good."

"Do you buy this story about a capsized boat and the husband who drowned?"

Hal thought for a moment. He gestured vaguely with one hand.

"What's it matter? After all, it's not that important. It's a plausible enough story and you can't ask any more, not even of a story..."

"I could hear her breathing in the dark..." said Frank dreamily. "And I wanted to get up and go and press my face down on her mouth..."

"You're not the only one."

"What! You too?"

"And how! I swear, if you hadn't been there, I'd have had me some fun. Quality goods and tasty with it!"

"You've got it bad!" laughed Frank.

But his laughter jarred and sounded false.

"You think so?"

"Well, I mean to say… She's been a widow ever since yesterday…"

"Widows," sniggered Hal, "are a like fish: mustn't wait too long before you gobble them up!"

"So you want her yourself, you old goat?"

Frank's face was bright red—and it wasn't on account of his temperature.

"And you don't?" asked Hal.

"Leave me out of it. For the moment, I'm blind."

"So what? Making love is something that's usually done in the dark!"

Frank stood next to the woman, whom he could vaguely make out through the thick fog which enveloped her.

"The way things are going," he said, "I'd be surprised if she stays prissy for long."

The still-sleeping woman sighed deeply.

"Was that her?" asked Frank.

"Yes. She's starting to wake up."

"And to think I can't see it! What's she doing?"

Hal had moved nearer to the blonde woman. He stood watching her with some satisfaction, with his lips drawn back over his sharp teeth.

"She's doing what all women do when they wake up," he said quietly. "She looks as if she's dreaming."

"And to think I can't see it! I can't see it!" said Frank, almost weeping while he desperately screwed up his eyes. "I could kill myself!"

"Cheer up! Mustn't start getting gloomy ideas!" said Hal in an effort to soothe his friend.

"Gloomy ideas! Brother, you said it!"

The woman was now staring at them in silence. She was hollow-cheeked with grief.

"Still, it's not everything," muttered Hal. "I'm going to make some coffee."

He leant over her:

"What's your name?" he asked.

She answered:

"Dora."

"Sounds like someone in the films," said Frank. "Still, some people like that sort of thing…"

Hal leant down farther. There was a glint in his eye. Dora did not pull away from him. She seemed transfixed.

Delicately he kissed her on the mouth.

Frank could not hear anything and felt anxious.

"What the hell are you two up to now?"

The kiss went on and on. Though it was not really a kiss, for it was one-way traffic. Hal gave it; Dora endured it.

Frank started getting very jumpy.

"What are you up to? What are you doing?"

"We're looking at you," answered Hal. "We've both got eyes, so why shouldn't we make the most of them?"

"You swine!…" cried Frank. "You're mocking me… But usually it's the deaf who get laughed at, not the blind!"

"But you're not blind," said Hal. "Don't exaggerate. Don't lay it on so thick."

"OK, OK!" said Frank, feeling crushed. "So I'm not blind, you're right. It's just that I can't see!"

PART IV

The Beast

15

The days that followed were as strange as those which had preceded Dora's arrival on the island. The three self-exiled castaways led a life not unlike that of campers. Dora seemed resigned to her fate. She had lost heart but put a brave face on things and submitted to the life imposed on her by the two men. They never let each other stray very far. When Hal went fishing for crabs or shrimps, Frank and the young woman went with him. They prepared their meals together and played pointless games using flat stones as a substitute for quoits. Dora never cried now, never spoke about her boating accident, and gave no indication that she would try to return to the mainland. All three, on the basis of a perfect tacit agreement, negotiated this dead time the way a thrown object works its way across its trajectory.

Then, when three days had passed, the climate of absolute peace changed. More precisely, after the end of the third night. For if intangible bonds of friendship were created during the days, the nights imperceptibly undid them again. It seemed as though the breathing of the three occupants of the hut could not be aligned harmoniously. There was a break in rhythm, a break in *the* rhythm of their three-person existence. The two men tossed and turned on their seaweed beds, heaving sighs, muttering confused words, while Dora never stirred. A tense atmosphere of repressed sensuality lay heavy on the hut. Frank did not sleep because he wanted to keep an eye on Hal. And Hal struggled to keep awake so that he could check on the behaviour of his partner. Each was afraid that the other would follow the instinct which lurked inside him. Whenever either of them made a movement, the other was immediately on full alert.

Each despised the other for being kept awake. Gossamer threads of hate spread in their souls, and, at first light, when with faces etched with insomnia they exchanged the first glance of the day, they felt the urge to leap on each other like enraged wild beasts.

Frank's wound was now markedly improved. His eyesight was quickly returning. There were periods of blurred vision and others, longer for the most part, when he could see almost normally.

Now, on the third night after Dora arrived, Frank, for all his resilience, fell into a deep sleep the moment he lay down. Hal felt his heart race at the thought that a sudden intimacy had sprung up between him and Dora.

He sighed softly. Without warning, the woman got up and tiptoed to the door.

"Where are you going?" whispered Hal.

"Outside…" she said. "It's too hot in here. I can't sleep."

She left without closing the door behind her. Through it, he saw her walk away. He leapt to his feet.

"Hey!" he said as he left the hut in her wake. "Not so fast, lady!"

She went on walking quickly towards the sea. He had to run to catch up with her.

"Thinking of taking a dip?"

"Why not?"

"Not many people go swimming at midnight…" said Hal sarcastically. "But if there's two of them, it's more fun!"

Dora did not respond. The tide was high and there was not much of the beach left. She took off her plimsolls and walked into the water.

But the water was cold and she beat a hasty retreat.

"No need to be shy, girl, not at this time of night!"

"Oh, be quiet," she said with a sigh. "You're getting on my nerves…"

"Is that so?"

"Yes. Do you think this idiotic situation can last much longer?"

"What do you reckon yourself?" asked Hal.

"I think it's totally and utterly idiotic."

He slid one arm along her bare shoulder, which was just touching his. The soft, warm feel of that silky skin made him tremble. His calloused hand tightened around the woman's arm.

He pulled her to him roughly. Indifferent, she did not not react.

"What's the matter, Dora?" asked Hal.

Then he gave a start on seeing the figure of Frank standing before them. He was leaning motionless against a rock, with his hands on his hips. His weak eyes blinked.

"All lovey-dovey, are we?" he asked.

Dora pulled away from Hal and headed back to the hut.

"I asked you a question," repeated Frank.

Hal had never seen so much rage in a man's eyes.

"And I won't answer it because it's a stupid question," he said. "You stand there, blowing a fuse because I try to make it with little Miss Chickadee… It's only human nature, isn't it? That first day, you yourself told me—"

"I don't give a damn about what I told you that first day!" snarled Frank. "There's no more first day! There's only nights now! Steamy nights that make me feel like I'm burning up all over."

"I know…" said Hal with a sigh. "It's the same with me. What do you expect? Think you're the only man here?"

They made their way back to the hut. The island was beginning to feel too small for them.

"We ought to be thinking of getting out of here now that you're on the mend," said Hal. "The hunt must have died down a lot in the last week, since we gave them the slip! And between you and me, I'm beginning to have seafood coming out of my ears!"

"We'll think about it," promised Frank. "You're right, amigo. Three of us here is getting too hard to bear!"

16

Frank was shelling crabs and Dora was busy boiling water. Hal had gone to gather dead wood in the tiny copse. This was becoming no easy task because, in their few days there, they had burnt all the dry brushwood which had been lying around on the island's short grass. Suddenly Hal burst through the door empty-handed.

"You haven't..." began Frank.

Hal advanced. He looked thoughtful.

"The revolver's gone," he said.

"What?" said Frank.

"I always carried it with me, in my jacket pocket... Then, as I was scouting round for wood, I noticed it wasn't there any longer!"

"You lost it?"

"That's what I thought at first," said Hal with a scowl.

"What do you mean it was what you thought at first?"

"I looked everywhere. On the short grass it's not hard to spot something black like a revolver. I saw nothing! Zilch!"

"But..." began Frank.

"But nothing," said Hal. "The plain fact is, I haven't got it any more... And I think that's a bit screwy... Don't you?"

Frank shrugged his shoulders.

"Couldn't you have dropped it when you were looking for crabs?"

"I wasn't wearing my jacket..."

"You probably lost it yesterday..."

"Nope. I had it this morning..."

Frank tossed a crab into the bucket of water.

"So what do you reckon?" he said.

"I reckon," said Hal, "that it isn't as far away as you might think. Somebody stole it from me."

Frank automatically looked at Dora.

"Somebody?"

"Somebody who happened to have bullets, for instance? Somebody who might find it useful to have a weapon."

Frank leapt up and grabbed his friend by the collar.

"So basically you're accusing me of stealing the gun, right?"

"Basically, yes!"

Frank shook his head.

"Well, you'd better get that stupid idea out of your system pronto, pal. I didn't take the revolver."

He tapped his inside pocket.

"Having the bullets is my insurance."

His face went suddenly tense; his hand stopped moving. Then feverishly he patted his pockets.

"The bullets!" gasped Frank. "The bullets!"

He rapidly searched through his clothes. His fingers shook with impatience. When he finished, he began again, more systematically. Hal frowned as he watched him.

"So you've lost them too?"

"Yes… Yes…"

Frank took his hand out of his jacket. He turned towards Hal. His eyes were livid with fury.

"It was you," he said, the accusation coming from somewhere deep in his throat.

"Obviously," smiled Hal. "To console myself for the loss of the gun, I stole the bullets from you!"

Frank grabbed him by both arms.

"It's not true! You didn't lose the gun! You hid it some-where after stealing the bullets off me. You're trying to divert suspicion away from yourself by claiming I stole it! I can see right through you, Hal! I'm not in the dark any more. I can see through your dirty little game!"

"That's enough!" thundered Hal. "It's you, you're trying to pull the wool over my eyes! It was you who took the gun off me and stashed it someplace with your bullets… But you're not going to get away with this. You're going to give it back! The whole caboodle—bullets and all!"

He was pale and spat the words into his partner's contorted face. Frank blinked first and took one step back.

"Who do you think you are?" he spluttered. "I never came across a son of a bitch like you! You're coming on a bit strong, Hal, you really are!"

"And on top of it all, now he takes me for a fool!" said Hal, almost to himself.

Dora had abandoned the fire to watch the two men engag-ing in their shouting match. She opened her vaguely disbe-lieving eyes, not understanding why they were going for each other like two rutting stags.

"Give me the gun back!" cried Hal.

"No, you're going to give it back to me, you dirty rat!"

Hal started to walk away, with his head down, but then cannoned into Frank. Frank took the hit in the forehead and a spurt of purple obscured his eyesight. He thought he had gone blind again and raised one hand to his wound.

"Aah!" he growled. "What did you do that for, Hal?"

Hal's rage subsided a little.

"Because, Frank, there isn't a bigger liar than you anywhere on the planet... Come on, hand the gun over and we'll say no more about it!"

Frank straightened up but kept his head bowed. Golden lights flashed and whirled in his eyes, but his sight was clearing and already he felt reassured. But he'd had a scare and his fear kept his anger high.

"You're pathetic, Hal," he said. "You know very well I didn't take the shooter and also that you've got the shells. And now you go and head-butt me right on my wound! I never had you down as a coward... All right, you can keep your gun... And if it makes you happy, you can put a bullet in my head—I'm so sick of you it would be a blessing..."

He walked out. Hal watched him go and shrugged his shoulders.

Then he turned to Dora:

"Sorry about the floor show. It's a while since the pair of us argued—we've missed it!"

She leant over her fire which was going out for lack of fuel.

"It's curious," she said after a moment, after she'd blown on the embers. "Anyone would think the two of you were afraid of each other."

Hal clenched his fists.

"Not true... You don't know what you're talking about."

"Fine, so it's not true," she said.

Outside, the weather was very bad. The wind was gusting and from time to time large clouds emptied themselves like split wineskins.

Hal watched Frank, who was dawdling along the beach. He was torn between wanting to run after him and say sorry for butting him and the urge to make the most of his absence to cosy up to Dora. In the end, the flesh proved stronger than finer feelings.

"With you around," he said, going up to her, "how do you expect men to get on with each other?"

She looked him up and down with some apprehension. He opened his arms but she stood motionless by her saucepan, from which little gasps of steam were now escaping…

"You've got the knack of getting under a man's skin…" said Hal. "When I look at you, it's like I'm standing in the middle of a blazing house—do you understand what I'm saying?"

"Go and fetch some wood, or we'll not be able to cook the meal!"

He tried to kiss her but she wriggled in his arms like an eel.

"Aw, come on!" said Hal. "What's wrong?"

"Just go and get the wood instead of playing the fool…"

Hal lowered his arms and went outside.

From where he was by the water's edge, Frank saw his partner making for the small copse. He told himself that here was the ideal opportunity for another attempt at a quiet chat with Dora. Until now, he hadn't been able to summon up enough courage to speak to her, but after what had happened he felt no loyalty to his companion. Hal was a dirty rat.

He almost ran towards the hut. Dora saw him heading towards her looking very determined.

"Did he hurt you?" she asked.

"He sure did! A head-butt that would have felled an ox… Caught me on my wound… It must look a pretty nasty mess now, right?"

She peered at it, then pulled a face.

"It's opened up again."

"The swine!" growled Frank.

He reached out and caught Dora by the waistband of her shorts. He drew her to him, released her shorts and encircled her with a backward sweep of his arm. He was strong. The young woman's body arched and he pressed her eagerly to him.

"My, such ardour in one of our walking wounded!" she murmured.

"Shut up," whispered Frank.

He sought Dora's lips. She turned her head away at the last moment to deprive him of them. He became more insistent. The touch of her bare legs, of her body—it felt so alive, so supple, so warm—inflamed him.

Losing interest in finding her mouth, he bit her on the neck with such fire that she gave a brief cry of pain and sensuality.

With his free hand, he caressed whatever it encountered in his wild excitement, fondling a breast, a thigh… He could hardly breathe, so great was his desire.

"I want you! I want you!"

He was almost weeping now. All pain had vanished from his face.

The door slammed. Hal slung an armful of wood across the hut. He put his hands on his hips and, with an ugly look in his eyes, stared at the entwined couple.

Frank swung round partly so that he could see his partner. Without taking his eyes off him he kissed Dora, almost forcing himself on her. Hal did not flinch. Frank released the woman and sat down. Hal shook the rain off his drenched clothes.

"It's coming down so hard that you wouldn't even send a cop out in it," he said.

17

Towards evening, the storm blew itself out and pink clouds began floating across the now-quiet sky. The three occupants of the island did not exchange a single word until darkness fell. They all went about their several tasks and thought separate thoughts.

They each nursed a dark resentment and resolutely hated each other without making any attempt to disguise the fact.

They went to bed early without saying goodnight to each other. They lay down on their seaweed beds at three different points of the shack and sought sleep. This they did with a savage determination to find it at any price and forget their predicament.

They were all conscious that they bore some responsibility for creating the tension, which made them feel more isolated than the fact of being together on an island.

For a considerable time, their jangled nerves made the musty seaweed rustle. There was much sighing… much clearing of throats… then their regular breathing was synchronized, while in the now-clear sky the moon travelled along its pale parabola above the waves.

Frank gave a sudden start. A golden ray of light was slanting through a crack in the hut. It fell directly onto his left eye. It was a rare and gratifying experience to be woken by the sun. For a brief moment, he savoured its dazzling caress. Then he turned his head and saw Hal asleep at the other end of the hut. He looked like a gun dog in repose and was breathing noisily.

Frank watched him without saying a word. He felt something akin to tenderness for his comrade. A tenderness curiously tinged with hatred. Or rather no: he just hated him affectionately, that was it!

He gave an imperceptible shrug. A need to make love gouged his flesh like a knife digging into an unripe fruit. He turned automatically to where Dora slept. She wasn't there. Frank stood up and crossed to the door. The island was bathed by the sun in a watery luminosity, like light in an aquarium. He looked right and left but could not see Dora anywhere. Her absence was like a physical pain.

"Hal," he shouted. "Wake up!"

Hal blinked.

He propped himself up on one elbow and yawned like a lion while looking uncertainly at his companion.

"You were right to wake me," he said. "I was dreaming I was in jail, a jail that was worse even than solitary in the slammer…"

Frank cut him short: "Dora's gone!"

Hal sat up.

"What?"

"Look! She's not here!"

"She'll have gone down to the sea."

"Yeah, but if she has I can't see her."

Hal ran outside. Then he sped off towards the copse, because it was the highest point on the island. From that knoll he would have an all-round view… Frank caught up with him.

"See? She really has gone," he said. "She'll have made up her mind because of the stupid way we carried on yesterday.

She took advantage of the high tide… You can see it's right up… It's a mess!… Either she's drowned or else she's raised the alarm. I tell you, we'll have the cops around our necks!… We'll get nicked! Let's hope she got drowned…"

"Oh, give it a rest, will you?" said Hal. "What's the use of getting all worked up about it?"

He scanned the sea separating them from the mainland. It was rucked with waves and white horses. There was no way a solitary swimmer could be seen in that grey expanse in perpetual motion without the use of a pair of powerful high-magnification binoculars.

Hal was thinking. Two deep lines appeared on his forehead.

"It's strange…" he said. "Why would she want to leave?"

"Why would she want to stay? Do you think being stuck here is much of a life? What are we going to do, Hal? Oh God! Let's hope the bitch got drowned!"

Hal walked back down to the hut. He didn't seem convinced that Dora had skipped out on them. Frank called out to him:

"Hey! What are we going to do?"

"Nothing for the moment," Hal shouted back. "We'll have to see."

"See what?"

"We'll just have to see… Just shut up for a minute, will you?"

"If that's the way you want it… Let's just sit and wait for the cops to show up since that's what you want… But I'm warning you, if I see them turning up I'll take my chances in the drink."

"OK."

Frank stopped running after his partner and went down to the beach. When he got there he burst out laughing. Dora was there, not swimming but floating, with her hands behind her head. A rock had had hidden her from Hal's anxious scrutiny.

He was so happy that his legs almost gave way under him. He approached her and understood why she had chosen her spot in the lee of the rock: she was naked.

When she caught sight of Frank, she gave a little scream.

"Go away," she said.

"Nothing doing! This is too good to miss…"

"Please! Don't be such a boor! You can see very well that I have no clothes on… I wanted to take a bath and…"

There was a strange look in Frank's eye. He waded into the water up to his knees without removing his shoes or trousers.

"Of course you did, a bath…" he stammered as if hypnotized. He leant over Dora. She tried to push him away but lost her balance, capsized and went under.

She cried out through the water, making a ridiculous gargling sound. Her head emerged. She gasped for air. Frank pulled her roughly by one arm. She rose from the waves like some Danish goddess, proud and beautiful, panting for breath.

Frank grabbed her round the waist and dragged her back to the sand. She fought; she screamed; she lashed out at him, but he ignored her fists. On the contrary, the way she kicked and screeched like any woman being assaulted stoked his desire to a high pitch. She twisted her head and bit him deeply on the forearm: all he felt was a mild discomfort. He dumped her unceremoniously on the ground and threw himself on her, maddened by the need to possess her body, which streamed with water and bucked and heaved in an effort to escape from him.

He did not speak. Teeth gritted and glassy-eyed, he breathed through his nose and his furious actions followed a certain method.

He had forgotten that Hal was not far away. And now Hal came running like a madman, with his fists clenched.

When he was standing over the couple, he bellowed:

"Let her go, you animal! Now!"

He dug his boot several times into Frank's back. The kicking shook Frank out of his private world. He tore himself away from his prey and whipped round. He was raving. A fine thread of spittle oozed from the corners of his lips.

"You disgust me!..." cried Hal. "You're a real scumbag! You're like a dog! An old, impotent dog!"

Frank raised his fist and brought it down on Hal's cheek. Hal staggered, regained his balance and threw a fierce right cross, which Frank narrowly dodged. Now the fight was really on. It wasn't a brawl, but a duel to the death. Dora slipped into her shorts and sailor's jersey before standing up to watch the two opponents. They were now grappling wildly with each other, grunting as they rolled over and over on the beach. Then they let go of each other and scrambled immediately to their feet like perfectly coordinated duettists.

Then the punches started flying thick and fast. They were evenly matched. Hal was visibly stronger than Frank, but in Frank's favour was his intense fury.

There came a moment when he sidestepped a lunge by his opponent and landed a fearsome hook to his liver. Hal went down like a log on the sand and stayed there without moving, face down, one foot in the water and one hand clutching a pebble.

Frank wiped away the blood that was pouring down his face. He suddenly felt desperately tired and utterly weary. Everything around him was becoming blurred again.

"My eyes must have taken a direct hit," he thought.

He turned to Dora but inferred her presence rather than saw her. She was no more than a shimmering reflection in his eyes, a shape with wavy outlines… He put his hand over his eyes so that he would not see the unsteady universe which was shaking like jelly.

"God, it hurts!" murmured Frank. "This time I really am going blind, I'm sure of it."

Swaying like a drunk, he staggered back to the hut and collapsed onto the wooden bench. He laid his head on one folded arm and sank into a comatose darkness. Gradually his body woke to a world of suffering. With every passing minute new pains caused by the punches he had taken declared themselves… He was done in.

Dora stared at Hal, who lay without moving on the sand. His face was also all bloodied. His split lips were bleeding profusely and a red stain spread out over the thirsty sand.

She knelt by him and gently stroked the bushy hair of the fallen man.

She took hold of one shoulder and pushed in an effort to turn him onto his back. Hal gave a sigh and blinked his eyes… His lips had tripled in size.

"The swine…" he spluttered painfully.

Dora leant over him and kissed that monstrous mouth. The kiss tasted of blood. When she straightened up her own lips were red with Hal's blood.

"We've got to leave," she said in a determined voice. "The best thing would be to put an end to this."

Hal got onto his knees. They both remained for a few moments in that position, like a pair of bookends, face to face, looking intently at each other.

"Yeah, let's get out of here," said Hal.

"The mainland is a fair way off, so we'll get a wooden bench and use that as a float. We'll hang on behind it and paddle with our feet. That'll be the easiest way."

"If you say so…" He added: "You think of everything!"

"I leave no stone unturned!" said Dora.

She walked to the strip of short grass at the edge of the beach and raised a flat rock. She slid her hand into the deepish cavity under it and pulled out a piece of cloth, which she proceeded to unfold.

Hal watched her, intrigued.

"What's that?" he asked.

She pulled the revolver from the cloth.

"It's this."

Bemused, he shook his head.

"So it was you who?…"

"Here's the proof…"

"What about the bullets?"

"In the chamber…"

"So you—"

"I removed from each of you the two separate components which, together, result in a loaded revolver…"

"You take the biscuit! You really do!"

It was all he could find to say. As he dabbed at his lips, he shook his head and rolled his eyes in amazement.

"Aren't you just the…"

He broke off when he saw her turn and head away in the direction of the hut. She walked slowly, the gun swinging at the end of her arm.

"Where are you going?" he suddenly called out.

She continued walking without turning round. Again Hal asked:

"Where are you going, Dora?"

But the only reply he got was the woman's back and her hand wrapped round the butt of the revolver. Then he understood.

"No, no!" he cried, at first to himself.

Then he got to his feet.

"No, Dora!… Listen…"

He continued to call in a clipped voice which passed between his enormous gashed lips with some difficulty.

"Listen, Dora… You mustn't… You mustn't… I don't want you to…"

He began to run, got ahead of her and started walking backwards in front of her while pleading with her in a hushed, urgent voice.

"Frank and me have been through too much…"

"You men," she spat contemptuously, "all that matters to you is friendship!"

He went on, almost sobbing now:

"We've bled together… killed together! Doesn't that count for anything?"

She saw tears in his eyes. Large, man-sized tears which were too embarrassed to fall.

She continued to stride towards the hut.

His stopped, his arms stretched wide.

"I'm telling you I don't want this! I won't have it!"

Dora raised the gun. Hal stared at the barrel, which was being aimed at him. He stepped back half a pace.

"Not afraid, are you?" she asked.

"When people have got a gun pointing at them, they get a bit nervous. It's only human nature."

"True," agreed Dora. "And when people have got their finger on a trigger, they become very powerful, which is also only human nature. It's as if you're holding a magic wand... You make a wish and it's answered straight away."

"Give it to me! A gun isn't a suitable thing for a woman..."

"It's suitable for anyone who needs one."

Hal sobbed: "Don't kill him! Please!... I'm begging you!"

She waved him to one side and continued walking towards the hut.

"So you feel that strongly about him?"

"Yes! We've both knocked each other about too much... That leaves a mark on two men! Too ready with our fists... Hammered each other too much... Hated each other too much!... Hatred like ours, Dora, is stronger than just affection, it goes much deeper!"

They said nothing more until they got to the hut. He followed at a distance, completely spent. Dora stood in the doorway. Three metres from her was Frank's back. It was broad and made a tempting target. Dora raised the gun and held it at arm's length. She closed one eye and looked through the foresight, drawing a bead on the centre of the enormous target.

"No!" screamed Hal.

He threw himself on her extended arm. The gun went off. The bullet ended up in the door frame. Frank jumped up and spun round. He had remained in darkness for too long and could see absolutely nothing!

"What's going on?" he said breathlessly.

Hal twisted Dora's arm. When the revolver fell to the floor he bent down lithely, gathered it up and with one incredibly rapid movement of his hand put a bullet into her temple.

Dora closed her eyes as if the shot had just grazed her. Then she toppled forward. Hal slowed her fall. Then he was holding the smoking gun and had no idea what to do next.

Frank blinked... Daylight was seeping imperceptibly into his eyes. He became gradually aware of the outlines of things. He made out Dora's lifeless body through a violet haze.

"Dora!" he called. "Dora!"

"Shut your mouth!" whispered Hal. "She's dead!"

"What did you say?"

"Dead! Got that? Done for, departed, permanent nothing!"

"You killed her..." stammered Frank. "You lousy swine! You killed her!... What the hell did you go and do that for, eh?"

Feeling his way forward, he grasped his adversary by his clothes and shook him furiously.

"I want to know... Why did you kill her? You were jealous, was that it? You were jealous because I wanted her and because in the end I'd have had her...

"And the revolver! You had it, didn't you, you rat? And the bullets! My bullets! And you accused me... You... Oh, it's not true, is it, that a worm like you could?... How come such a piece of low-down trash as you was ever born?..."

He was screaming into Hal's face, which at last he could make out. He went on shaking him as he spoke.

"But she was going to plug you, Frank!" cried Hal. "She's the one who stole the gun and the shells! She'd hidden the piece under a rock, in a hole... I swear! It's God's honest truth, Frank!... You've got to believe me!"

You're lying! You killed her because you were jealous... So jealous it hurt! And now you're going to shoot me too!"

"No, Frank... I'm not going to shoot you!... I tell you, its the very opposite..."

"Your hands! Come on, give me your hands!"

"If it's the piece you want, here it is, but stop yelling so much!"

Frank reached hungrily for the ridged butt. The revolver was warm—it could have been a small, living animal. He felt calmer.

"She wanted to—" persisted Hal.

"Shut up! I can't bear to hear you speak any more. Your voice offends me! I know that what you wanted all along was to shoot somebody! I know it for a fact... Murderers are always itching to kill! It's as if they're hungry for death... And I know what murderers are like, Hal..."

"Of course you do," said Hal.

"And do you know how I know what they're like?"

"Sure I do, Frank..."

"So tell me, you bastard!"

"Because you're a cop," murmured Hal sadly.

"You bet I am," said Frank.

Hal gave a shrug… He put his hands in his pockets. The blood had dried on his lips, forming a shiny crust, like red varnish.

"I knew it," he sighed, "the moment we walked into that cell together! My instinct warned me you were the law… a secret-service agent… I went on believing it even after I saw you gunning those screws down… You sure paid your dues!"

"I paid what I had to," said Frank.

"And now you're blind as a bat, you slimy bastard!…"

"Shut your mouth!" said Frank.

He leant back against the hut. He was very pale and his nose looked pinched. Hal took a quick step forward.

"Not feeling too good, Frank?"

"It's nothing…" said Frank. "I just felt a bit dizzy…"

"Pull yourself together," pleaded Hal. "I don't want you dying on me… I like you a lot, Frank… even though you're a cop. There are times when it don't matter any more if you're a cop or a bad guy! Are you listening to me?"

He shook him; there were tears in his eyes.

"For us two," he went on, "which side of the fence we're on doesn't matter any more. Look, there aren't any fences any more! We're just a couple of guys, Franky boy! Just two poor saps adrift in the lowest depths of hell!"

He fell silent, his chest raw from shouting.

"There's still one bullet left, right?" asked Frank, holding up the revolver.

"Yeah, Frank. Just the one."

"Good," said Frank in a quiet voice. "It's got your name on it."

He made an effort to see where Hal was. But his vision was still blurred. Just grey shapes with wavy edges, and too bright, as usual…

"You're crazy!" cried Hal. "I told you how she was going to put a bullet in your hide and that it was me who—"

"Pretty woman, isn't she?" murmured Frank.

Hal look down at Dora's lifeless body.

"Even prettier now she's dead."

Frank tried to take deep breaths. He had to ease the weight on his chest before he could speak again.

For he still had something else, something crucial to say: he had to explain something serious.

"Listen, Hal," he began.

He felt Hal was giving him his full attention.

"Listen," he resumed, "I'm going to shoot you... No, don't argue, Hal... Try to understand..."

"I understand," said Hal.

"You wouldn't want all we've lived through to have been for nothing, would you, Hal?... There's never been anything like it; it was diabolical, when you think... The only way it can be justified is for me to shoot you with this last bullet... If it were up to me, Hal, I'd shoot wide... Problem is, this bullet doesn't belong to me. It belongs to society and I can't just do whatever I like with it... Do you... Do you understand what I'm saying?"

Hal felt two tears roll down his bruised cheeks.

"Yes, Frank, I understand..."

"Fine... That's good."

Frank raised the gun.

"Wait a minute," murmured Hal. "I've got something to tell you too... It's quite true, Frank, that she wanted to bump you off... It's also true that she hid the shooter..."

Frank believed him.

"OK."

"Yeah, and you know why?"

"No," said Frank, gripped by a sudden feeling of unease.

"Because she was my chief!"

"What did you say?"

"You heard… though it would take the skin off my voice box to say it again… She was the overall head of the section in France… When I was arrested she managed to get a message through to me. I remember it exactly: 'A cop will come soon and help you to escape.' She was a very smart lady and she anticipated everything.

"Later she smuggled another message in to me…"

"When?"

"When we were banged up in jail."

Frank shook his head.

"Do you think I'm a fool?"

"No… She'd bribed one of the screws and while I was in the slammer…"

Hal ran a damp hand through his hair.

"Didn't you suspect anything when we found that motorboat all ready to go? Normally they're securely locked up… And the same goes for just happening to come across a gutsy lady who was hosting a party… A doll who got us out of a jam… Didn't any of that surprise you?"

Frank shook his head.

"So why did we have to make a quick getaway from her place? All you had to do was put a slug in me and then go on your way."

Hal looked at the floor.

"That was what I was supposed to do, Frank: lead you away

from the house and bump you off. But I couldn't bring myself to do it… Then we fetched up here… She came looking for us…"

"Thanks, Hal," said Frank. "Thanks for everything… Now go—get out of here. I'll count to three. Try to dodge the last bullet in the chamber! Good luck, pal, and take care of yourself!"

Hal sensed that there was nothing more to be said. With a sigh, he turned on his heel and walked away slowly.

Frank raised the gun and pointed it at random. His eyesight was still blurred. To him, Hal was just a moving blot. He hesitated, then counted silently to three.

"Oh God," he prayed, "make me miss!"

He pulled the trigger with a crisp action.

The shot made the gun jump in his hand. He let it drop to the ground. He did not dare move from the spot… He looked but could only make out the grey shape of his comrade. He saw that the shape was upright and his heart leapt with joy.

"Hal!" he called softly. "Hal!"

There was no answer. But the figure was still standing. Frank began walking towards it. Then he saw the grey shape measure its length silently on the sparse grass.

"Hal! Hal!"

He was shouting now… Then he was running. He stumbled over his friend and dropped to his knees.

"Did I hit you?" he panted. "Tell me, Hal, did I wing you? Come on, stop playing the fool, Hal! Get up! Get up!… Please!"

He patted the tall body on the ground in front of him… Suddenly it had become just an inert mass.

He ran his hand over Hal's clothes, searching for his chest… He finally found his heart… a barely detectable beat… as faint and fitful as the ticking of a faulty wristwatch which has been shaken and, for just a few moments, seems to be working normally.

"Hal!"

His hand gently rubbed the heart that had run its course.

"Oh Hal, I feel so close to you, Hal!… You're my best friend… my brother… I'm so sorry! Please forgive me! Can you hear me? I need you to hear me!…"

Frank's fingers felt the heart stop beating. Then all that remained was just a hideous absence.

Slowly Frank's head sank down until it came to rest on that dead chest. He began to cry.

Yes, I wept.

I'm not ashamed to say it. Tears like those are the noblest that a man can shed. They are what make a man a man.

I wept over the carcase of a bad man because I'd just understood a great truth: there are no bad men...

He'd saved my life twice; he had sacrificed his own self-interest and his ideology, his love, his past to me... And yet a man of action remains loyal to the laws he has lived by. A man as vibrantly alive as Hal stays true to his passions... And everyone cherishes his own past... That was a great gift he had taught me.

And in return I'd put a bullet in his back.

Listen, I'm going to admit something: when I pulled that trigger, I wasn't aiming at him. The more I think about it, the more convinced I am that I really wanted to waste the shot. But I hit him all the same because I couldn't see! *When anyone talks to you about destiny, you'll know now what it is...*

Destiny... is another word for life's irony, for the kicks in the teeth it administers when you least expect it... It's... It's life unvarnished... That's what it is!

Sometimes of an evening, before I settle myself for sleep, I think of that tiny island, somewhere off the beaten track, beyond those treacherous quicksands which are periodically covered by the sea. Yes... My thoughts turn to the island and the two others... Dora, with her blonde hair and bare, golden legs...

Dora with the violet eyes whose steady gaze was unnerving... Dora and Hal...

But he was something else.

I remember that the sky that morning was white. You know, the sort of sky on which you'd like to scrawl portents in feathery writing! A sky that would stir up humankind to fashion the world anew... or to put an end to it once and for all!

The Old Man was waiting for me in his hermetically sealed office. From close by came the screams of some suspect being beaten up.

"Here's my report," I muttered, putting a sheaf of paper on his desk.

He nodded.

Then I took a crumpled envelope from my pocket.

"I must give you this as well."

He understood at once. His grey wrinkles grew deeper.

"I suppose this is your resignation?"

"Yes, sir... I'm resigning."

He picked up the envelope, weighed it in his hand and smiled. Then he tore it in two, having no intention of opening it, to destroy it.

The guy in the next room gave a scream, the loudest yet.

"Sit down."

I made a gesture of refusal, I had words ready to object, but his piercing eyes were too much for me. After a while, I sat down.

And ever since then, life has gone on.

———

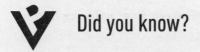 **Did you know?**

One of France's most prolific and popular post-war writers, Frédéric Dard wrote no fewer than 284 thrillers over his career, selling more than 200 million copies in France alone. The actual number of titles he authored is under dispute, as he wrote under at least 17 different aliases (including the wonderful Cornel Milk and l'Ange Noir).

Dard's most famous creation was San-Antonio, a James Bond-esque French secret agent, whose enormously popular adventures appeared under the San-Antonio pen name between 1949 and 2001. The thriller in your hands, however, is one of Dard's "novels of the night" – a run of stand-alone, dark psychological thrillers written by Dard in his prime, and considered by many to be his best work.

Dard was greatly influenced by the great Georges Simenon. A mutual respect developed between the two, and eventually Simenon agreed to let Dard adapt one of his books for the stage in 1953. Dard was also a famous inventor of words – in fact, he dreamt up so many words and phrases in his lifetime that a 'Dicodard' was recently published to list them all.

Dard's life was punctuated by drama; he attempted to hang himself when his first marriage ended, and in 1983 his daughter was kidnapped and held prisoner for 55 hours before being ransomed back to him for 2 million francs. He admitted afterwards that the experience traumatised him for ever, but he nonetheless used it as material for one of his later novels. This was typical of Dard, who drew heavily on his own life to fuel his extraordinary output of three to five novels every year. In fact, when contemplating his own death, Dard said his one regret was that he would not be able to write about it.

So, where do you go from here?

If you feel like another novel of the night, try Dard's *Bird in a Cage*, a brilliantly moody Parisian tale of suspense and murder.

Or for something even grittier, pick up a copy of Jonathan Ames' shocking and unputdownable debut thriller, *You Were Never Really Here*.

AVAILABLE AND COMING SOON
FROM PUSHKIN VERTIGO

Jonathan Ames

You Were Never Really Here

Augusto De Angelis

The Murdered Banker
The Mystery of the Three Orchids
The Hotel of the Three Roses

María Angélica Bosco

Death Going Down

Piero Chiara

The Disappearance of Signora
Giulia

Frédéric Dard

Bird in a Cage
Crush
The Wicked Go to Hell

Martin Holmén

Clinch

Alexander Lernet-Holenia

I Was Jack Mortimer

Boileau-Narcejac

Vertigo
She Who Was No More

Leo Perutz

Master of the Day of Judgment
Little Apple
St Peter's Snow

Soji Shimada

The Tokyo Zodiac Murders

Seishi Yokomizo

The Inugami Clan